LE1
FC
TALES

For Nigel & Judy

Some wee tales

from my

little corner of

Ireland - Enjoy!

Susie Minto

# LEITRIM

# FOLK TALES

SUSIE MINTO

ILLUSTRATED BY
TRACEY JEAN YAPPA

The
History
Press
Ireland

*With gratitude to every person who has shared any part of the road of life with me. Your stories and my stories combine to make me who I am, the sum of all of my experiences, friendships, relationships, stories. Without your presence, my story would not be the beautiful one that it is today. I am richly blessed.*

*And to Sophia, my feline muse, who keeps me peaceful!*

First published 2013

The History Press Ireland
50 City Quay
Dublin 2
Ireland
www.thehistorypress.ie

© Susie Minto, 2013
Illustrations © Tracey Jean Yappa

British Library Cataloguing in Publication Data.
A catalogue record for this book is available from the British Library.

ISBN 978 1 84588 759 9

Typesetting and origination by The History Press

# CONTENTS

# Acknowledgements

The Irish Folklore Commission put in place the makings of a world-class archive in 1937 when they joined forces with schools in the twenty-six counties of Ireland to enable pupils to collect material concerning local customs, traditions, stories, lore and much more. The returns were phenomenal – around 500,000 copybook pages of information, all handwritten in the beautiful stylised form of the late 1930s. Forty years later, the pages were put on microfilm and they are an invaluable resource across the counties.

I am grateful to Críostóir Mac Cárthaigh, archivist at the National Folklore Collection at University College Dublin (UCD), for guidance concerning the use of this material and for permission from his department to use several pieces directly as they appear in the archive, as well as to freely refer to many other stories from the collection.

The Local Studies staff of Ballinamore Library always found a seat for me beside a microfilm reader – even when I brought in my own footstool and lap-tray to ease strain in my neck!

Thanks to the authors and local historians I spoke to along the way, who gave me pointers and permission to use material they had researched and published.

To my friend, Ruth Marshall, who was simultaneously working on Clare Folk Tales – we were good sounding boards for each other.

For the inspired connection with Tracey Jean Yappa, who illustrated the stories. Thank you for 'seeing' the stories so well and for introducing me to the beauty of Benbo!

For friends in Ireland and beyond – you all played your part in keeping me inspired and committed to this project. Thank you!

The sources for all material are listed at the end of each chapter. A lot of the stories are developed and rewritten from material found in The Schools Manuscripts Collection (NFCS) held by UCD. In a number of instances, permission was granted to reproduce the material in full and this is clearly noted. The NFCS material is referenced using UCD's style, which includes the manuscript number and page, the teller, collector, school and teacher. In some instances not all the information was available.

# ABOUT
# THE AUTHOR

Born in Scotland to a British Canadian father and Middle Eastern Jewish mother, Susie inherited their nomadic spirit. She has lived in Scotland, England and Ireland and passed through many other countries. She counts people from many countries among her closest friends. After being told at twelve years old to speak less in class, she finds it humorous to think she gets paid for speaking now.

Susie's professional career began in print journalism, on a daily newspaper, and public relations. In 1992, she left her professional life and spent four years doing a full-time degree in theology and pastoral studies. This led to work as a course co-ordinator at the college where she studied. Then, storytelling entered her life and a mighty doorway swung wide open, calling her into the infinite possibility of the creative arts. She became the administrator of a national Christian storytelling initiative in England and attended as many storytelling workshops as she could, following her instincts into what was becoming a substantial change of life path. In 2003 she took the plunge, leaving behind, for the time being, the lifestyle of a secure salaried job to become a self-employed storyteller, winging it!

To add strings to her bow as she journeyed along, she did a course in therapeutic story work then a diploma in Steiner kindergarten education. The next training that fitted organically was in peace-building and community development, focussing on helping people to share their stories out of conflict experiences. This course was funded by the International Fund for Ireland. Most recently, Susie became an accredited facilitator of creative writing groups, using the Amherst Writers and Artists Method, as devised by Pat Schneider (*Writing Alone and with Others*, OUP) and she runs regular and occasional creative writing groups. Susie moved to Ireland in 2004 and has lived in County Leitrim since 2005.

# About
# the Illustrator

Tracey Jean Yappa is a graphic design artist and landscape painter. In early 1992 she moved to Leitrim from England, inspired by family stories of Irish ancestry and seeking a rural lifestyle. She now lives with her family on the lower slopes of Benbo Mountain, which features in many of the tales included in this book. An avid gardener and wildlife enthusiast, she also creates large-scale arts for street theatre and festivals with community groups of all ages, in and around Leitrim. It is a love of nature and mythology which is the inspiration for much of her work.

# INTRODUCTION

It is a road with many bends that we walk in life, never knowing what is around the corner or how one thing leads to another. Thus has been my journey with storytelling – I can pinpoint the exact position where my extraordinary new adventure with the oral tradition began, but I have no idea how the multitudinous roads I had previously travelled brought me to that point.

In 1998, whilst living in England, I was invited to be a steward at a storytelling venue at Greenbelt, a Christian arts festival. There is a long back-story to the path that led me there and it would take more than the rest of my years to attempt to map that out. Suffice to say, as I watched the beautiful transformation of the plain white marquee into a 'holy of holies' inner sanctum, with soft cushions and multicoloured saris draped as a thin veil of curtaining, my life changed – even before I heard the first story told. When I did hear the first, second, third … storytellers perform their captivating tales, nothing would ever be the same again for me.

Up to that point in my life – the tender age of forty-one – I had no recollection of having seen a live performance by a storyteller. That has to be an ironic claim for a person who was, according to some teasing friends, probably inoculated with a gramophone needle at birth. Talking was my life. So why hadn't I discovered the art-form? Stranger still, since I was a journalist on a regional newspaper in Scotland when the renaissance in storytelling was emerging in the 1970s and 1980s – yet I never wrote a story about storytelling, nor encountered the wonderful oral tradition in any way.

I am certain that our eyes are kept metaphorically closed until our time comes. I have no idea why my time came when it did but I knew it – and I say this consciously and carefully – I knew it as close as I can imagine what becoming pregnant must feel like. I used the terms associated with pregnancy and birth to describe then to friends my absolute sense that something new had been conceived in me. I told people it would impact my life so much that it would either be a hobby that would use up a lot of time or I would have to change my job. I knew it that well.

And what a peculiar road it has been since. No motorway from A to B, but a continuing journey of bends and twists, acquiring ever more strings to my creative bow, as well as a mixture of highs and lows on a personal level. The most profound aspect of this life change was moving from the head to the heart, from being in work that needed my thinking – my head energy – so much that I was mentally exhausted. Storytelling became a salve, a healing ointment to nourish my heart, to heal old, hidden wounds. It met me exactly when I needed its medicine. I breathed it in, it awoke my hitherto slumbering imagination and tapped into the infinite realm of ideas and creative suggestions that brought me work in schools, libraries, galleries and museums.

To begin with, I travelled the route of performance, but out of necessity (to protect my not-so-strong vocal chords), and for the inspired realisation that I wanted to help others to tap into their own slumbering imaginations and find their unique voices, I quickly made the transition towards creating workshops. The ideas rolled out and the work came in.

Early on the journey, I met an Irishman who loved his country's heritage of song and story. In 2004 I moved from Scotland to be with him in Ireland, choosing to invest my energies in building my new work in his country. Sadly, he passed away within a few years, yet I am still here, finding my story in another land, for the time being at least. He would be the happiest person on earth to see this book happening. He was my greatest fan!

It is thus a peculiar honour to be invited to compile a book of stories for the county that has been my adopted home for nine years. Being a 'blow in', to use the Irish vernacular, I didn't have a well-established repertoire bursting to be written down for this collection. In fact, I didn't have a single Leitrim story to tell. I had accumulated a fair sprinkling of quirky tales of humpbacks, fairies mending withered legs, enchanted cows, and shape-shifting hares and beetles from the rich gleanings of the main collectors such as Jeremiah Curtin, Lady Gregory, Joseph Jacobs and Crofton Croker – but none of these was placed in Leitrim.

So I had to begin at the beginning. My original plan had been to drive through as much of the land as possible, asking at all the little post offices for contacts of old folk in the area who were known to have some local stories. It was a noble plan, but circumstances prevented that and my story-gathering journey had to go by a different route.

I all but moved house into the Local Studies section of the Leitrim County Council Library HQ in Ballinamore. Many days of searching through the thousands of pages of microfiche from the Irish Folklore Commission's 1937 schools collection proved to be a fruitful starting ground to get me 'into' the county's personality. Local place-name books, parish story collections, the *Leitrim Guardian*, the internet – the marvellous internet – all swelled my bountiful harvest.

Layer by layer I dug into the depths of the county and found nuggets of stories from its mountains, loughs and misty hillsides. I was like a detective picking up leads, which multiplied as my newfound knowledge of the area grew. Stories met each other from all corners, no doubt deeply planted by the old traditions of the travelling seancaithe and scéalaí – the Tradition Bearers and Storytellers. The tales were a little different in some of their detail but they resonated from the same core: fairy charms, luck and success, greed and trickery, tragedy and victory, humour and heartache.

And now we arrive at the place where I courageously offer my gleanings to receptive readers. This baby has been in the womb for the full term and is ready to see the light of day; she can't stay a minute longer as she has so many stories to tell!

I shall say one more thing in closing. Back at that life-transforming crossroads in 1998 when I met a professional storyteller for the first time (even getting my imagination into that possibility was a stunning awakening – a professional storyteller!), the person I dared to speak to about what I was experiencing gave me what remains the most precious single piece of advice about storytelling and I pass it on in all my workshops. In reply to my question about how someone begins the journey of becoming a storyteller, she first of all suggested I read the deep work by Clarissa Pinkola Estés, *Women who Run with the Wolves* (Rider, 1992), as a way to begin to understand archetypes, which are at the heart of stories. The second – and most significant – part of her response was a heart-plea to listen to many storytellers, to read and research many stories and to notice which stories make a connection with me. Those would be the stories that I could tell best. It was strange at first but now I know it to be true – she warned me that a storyteller has to believe in the stories they tell because if they don't the audience can't either and they will feel betrayed. These words pierced me. My repertoire has stayed true to her words and I am all the richer for the deep nourishment I have received from the stories that I tell. I say to audiences that the stories nourish and heal me long before the words leave my lips.

Thus, I pass on this collection of Leitrim Folk Tales to the hearts, ears and eyes of all those who will receive them.

As for the road ahead for me, for you? Who knows? A few bends, a few twists, new friends, new stories …

*Susie Minto, 2013*

# LOVELY LEITRIM

Once upon a time, a Leitrim-born man living in New York wrote a song, as if in a dream, about the land he longed to see. It found its way back across the Atlantic, all the way to his home county and beyond, and began to be sung by popular request at country dances and musical gatherings. Tragically, the song's author died in 1947 and he didn't see his penned words rise to the very top of the British charts in the 1960s. He didn't know that it sold over one million copies worldwide, bringing tears to the eyes of nearly every Leitrim émigré who heard it played on a foreign shore, a long way from home.

The song, 'Lovely Leitrim', has almost mythical status in the county and it seems only right to include it at the beginning of this collection of stories from Leitrim, as it still has the effect of bringing people into a state of reverence and gentle patriotism when it is played and sung.

'Lovely Leitrim' was written by Philip Fitzpatrick, who was born in Aughavas in 1895. He emigrated to the US in the early 1930s and became a policeman with the New York Police Department. He was tragically killed, while off duty, during a robbery in a restaurant in 1947.

The song found its way into the Cunningham family, where a young lad called Larry heard his Ballinamuck-born mother sing it often. It appealed to him and when he and his dance band, The Mighty Avons, added it to their repertoire it began to take on a life of its own. The song put Larry Cunningham and his band at number one in the British pop music charts for four weeks in 1965. In late 1969, Larry left The Mighty Avons and merged with The Fairways to form Larry Cunningham and the Country Blue Boys. They continued to have top ten hits in the 1960s and 1970s, adding television appearances and international tours to their credit.

In the 1960s, the song composer's widow and two of his sons turned up at a venue in New York where Larry was performing. They gave him the handwritten original of the composition, which extended to six verses; Larry's recording was of four verses. Below are all six verses, reproduced in full with permission from Val Fitzpatrick, Mohill, a nephew of the late composer.

Whilst the composer and the singer who made the song so well-known are no longer alive (Larry Cunningham died in 2012) like a good story, the song lives on.

Last night I had a pleasant dream, I woke up with a smile;
I dreamt that I was back again in dear old Erin's Isle.
I thought I saw Lough Allen's banks in the valley down below,
It was my lovely Leitrim where the Shannon waters flow.

I stood enchanted by the scene of grandeur and delight
So headed on for Carrick town before the dark of night.
I passed Sheemore, that fairy hill where flowers wildly grow
And I saw the grave of Fionn MacCúil where the Shannon waters flow.

The next I saw was Fenagh town with her ancient abbey walls
Where the preaching of her holy monks re-echoes through her halls
I stood with reverence on the spot, reluctant for to go
From the town of saints and sages where the Shannon waters flow.

*My eyes are dim and wet with tears – I must be dreaming still.
I thought I saw those heroes who died on Selton Hill
The fog is lifting from the scene and I am forced to go
And leave this land so fair and grand where the Shannon waters flow.

*The English man drinks to the rose, the Scots man the Blue Bell,
Each sings his country's praises and great deeds of valour tell
But give me Ireland's Shamrock green that abundantly does grow
On the fertile fields of Leitrim where the Shannon waters flow.

I've travelled far through these fair lands, from the East unto the West
But of all the islands I have seen, I love my own the best.
And if ever I return again, there's one place I will go
It will be to lovely Leitrim, where the Shannon waters flow.

*The verses marked with an asterix were not included in Larry Cunningham's recording.

## REFERENCES

Larry Cunningham, 'My Leitrim', *Leitrim Guardian* 2003; Val Fitzpatrick, Mohill, a nephew of the composer, the late Philip Fitzpatrick; www.nypdangels.com/cop/cop.php?id=300.

# 1

# UNFATHOMABLE
# MONSTERS IN
# DEEP WATERS

Hailing as I do from Scotland, I grew up with many variations of the story of the Loch Ness monster. Do I believe the stories unconditionally because it is part of my cultural psyche? Do I concur with them as a mythical possibility alongside so many other unknowns in the worlds beyond what the naked eye can see? Or do I see them slightly cautiously, if not cynically, as a fine way for tourism in the Scottish Highlands to keep a healthy cash flow in visitor centres, B&Bs, hotels and restaurants, not to mention the tartan and plastic industries of tourist memorabilia? I can't say one way or another. Perhaps I'm pulled in all directions and none.

It is said that the first recorded sighting of a monster in Loch Ness was in AD 565, when followers of St Columba reportedly saw a monster in the Loch. Discussions continue well into our present century about its existence, as well as the possibility of other creatures thriving in waters that are deeper than human exploration has yet been able to plumb.

Nessie, as 'she' is affectionately known to tourists, is a cryptid, a term used by cryptozoologists to describe a hidden creature which might exist. To qualify as a cryptid, there needs to be some form of evidence of existence. This can mean being mentioned in folklore or that there have been 'sightings'. Explanations for monsters living in deep lakes are endless and include theories that they are large fish, optical illusions or massive underwater waves.

Here in Ireland the tourist industry is certainly not rolling in the cash for hard-pressed B&Bs by promoting its water monster heritage. There are no plastic Nessie equivalents for the tales of serpents carving river beds or of eels guarding treasures in deep lakes high up in the mountains. The tourist circuit doesn't include packed buses heading to glens, loughs and lonely hillsides to stand where such creatures are reputed to have been seen, or to follow the trail of other creatures which appeared in a more this-worldly guise – such as black horses and cows – arriving unexpectedly to the aid of farmers or poor folk.

Is this a lost opportunity for Ireland? Perhaps – or perhaps not. There are probably as many stories in Ireland as in Scotland about otherworldly sightings, except that here they are hiding in archives and scant published material, as deep as the lakes themselves, and not so easy to call to the surface.

However, one water creature's story that caught my fancy as I tracked down material for this collection is that of An Dobharchú (water hound).

## An Dobharchú

This tale is as mythical in proportion as it is in having considerable fact behind it, not least the now faint but still accessible carving on a gravestone in North Leitrim. The carving relates to an incident in September 1722, retold in incredible detail both in prose and poem form, the latter credited to an unidentified hedge school master. Sources suggest it may have been composed first in Irish and later translated. It was widely told and sung as a ballad at fairs in the area around Glenade Lake, the central scene of this strange event.

I am indebted to Sligo historian and writer Joe McGowan for his research on this story, and in giving me permission to reference his book, *Echoes of a Savage Land*, and his website, www.sligoheritage.com, from which I sourced the poem and the following supporting details.

The story tells of a fierce struggle to the death between the Mc Loughlin brothers of Glenade and 'that fierce brute the whistling Dobharchú'. The legend of An Dobharchú stems from the bestial murder of Grainne Ni Conalai at Glenade Lake on 24 September 1722. Some folk say she went to the lake to wash clothes; the ballad tells she went to bathe. Either way, when she failed to return, her husband, Traolach Mac Lochlainn, went to look for her. He was aghast when he found her body lying by the lake with the 'beast lying asleep on her mangled breast'.

This and the chase that ensued would have little credibility today were it not for the tombstone marking the grave of Grainne Ni Conalai that can still be seen at the old cemetery of Conwell, near Kinlough. Although worn smooth and less clear now, the carving is still visible and shows a strange beast being stabbed by a dagger. Local people claim a similar monument existed at one time not so far away in Kilroosk cemetery. Broken and lost around 1922, it may have been the inspiration for the Conwell memorial, or indeed evidence of yet another monster.

According to Patrick Doherty of Glenade, local lore records that the monster began to chase Traolach who galloped away on his steed, but the chase ended at Caiseal-bán (Cashelgarron) stone fort, when Mac Lochlainn was forced to stop at the blacksmith's to replace a lost horseshoe. When the enraged monster reached the forge the horse was hurriedly drawn across the entrance to form a barrier. Giving the terrified man a sword, the blacksmith advised him: 'When the creature charges the horse, he'll put his head right out through him. As soon as he does this you be quick and cut his head off.' Patrick insists the story's credibility is proven by the carved image engraved on Grainne Ni Conalai's tombstone in Conwell cemetery.

Cashelgarron stone fort still stands today, nestled under the sheltering prow of bare Benbulben's head. Both monster and horse are said to lie buried nearby.

The words of the poem reinforce Patrick's assertions. Joe notes that, even though the scribe's name is lost to us as well as the circumstances of his existence, his voice speaks eloquently across the centuries as clearly as if the words were penned yesterday. They are an articulate and enduring tribute to the event and to the poet's genius.

By Glenade Lake tradition tells, two hundred years ago
A thrilling scene enacted was, to which, as years unflow,
Old men and women still relate, and while relating dread
Some demon of its kind may yet be found within its bed.

It happened one McGloughlan lived close by the neighbouring shore,
A lovely spot, where fairies oft in rivalry wandered o'er,
A beauteous dell where prince and chief oft met in revelry
With Frenchmen bold and warriors old to hunt the wild boar, free.

He and his wife, Grace Connolly, lived there unknown to fame,
There [or 'Their']* years in peace, until one day from out the lakes there came
What brought a change in all [their bliss,] their home and prospects too
The water fiend, the enchanted being, the dreaded Dobharchú.

It was on a bright September morn, the sun scarce mountain-high,
No chill or damp was in the air, all nature seemed to vie
As if to render homage proud the cloudless sky above,
A day for mortals to discourse in luxury and love.

And whilst this gorgeous way of life in beauty did abound,
From out the vastness of this lake stole out the water hound,
And seized for victim her who shared McGloughlan's bed and board;
His loving wife, his more than life, whom almost he adored.

She having gone to bathe, it seems, within the water clear,
And not returning when she might, her husband, fraught with fear,
Hasting to where he her might find, when oh, to his surprise,
Her mangled form, still bleeding warm, lay stretched before his eyes.

Upon her bosom, snow-white once, but now besmeared with gore,
The Dobharchú reposing was, his surfeiting [now] being o'er.
Her bowels and entrails all around tinged with a reddish hue:
'Oh God,' he cried, ''tis hard to bear but what am I to do?'

He prayed for strength; the fiend lay still, he tottered like a child,
The blood of life within his veins surged rapidly and wild.
One long-lost glance at her he loved, then fast his footsteps turned
To home, while all his pent-up rage and passion fiercely burned.

He reached his house, he grasped his gun, which, clenched with nerves of steel,
He backwards sped, upraised his arm and then one piercing squeal
Was heard upon the balmy air. But hark! What's that which came
One moment next from out its depth as if revenge to claim!

The comrade of the dying fiend with whistles long and loud
Came nigh and nigher to the spot. McGloughlan, growing cowed
Rushed to his home, his neighbours called, their counsel asked, and flight
Was what they bade him do at once and not to wait 'til night.

He and his brother, sturdy pair, as brothers true when tried,
Their horses took, their home forsook and westward fast did ride.
One dagger sharp and long each man had for protection too
Fast pursued by that fierce brute, the whistling Dobharchú.

The rocks and dells rang with its yells, the eagles screamed in dread.
The ploughman left his horses lone, the fishes too, 'tis said,
'way from the mountain streams, though far, swam rushing to the sea;
And nature's laws did almost pause, for death or victory.

For twenty miles the gallant steeds the riders proudly bore
With mighty strain o'er hill and dale that ne'er was seen before.
The fiend, fast closing on their tracks, his dreaded cry more shrill;
'Twas 'Brothers try, we'll do or die, on Cashelgarron Hill.'

Dismounting from their panting steeds, they placed them one by one
Across the path in lengthways formed within the ancient dún,
And standing by the outmost horse, awaiting for their foe
Their daggers raised, their nerves they braced to strike that fatal blow.

Not long to wait for nose on trail the scenting hound arrived
And through the horses with a plunge to force himself he tried,
And just as through the outmost horse he plunged his head and
foremost part,
McGloughlan's dagger to the hilt lay buried in his heart.

'Thank God, thank God,' the brothers cried, in wildness and delight,
Our humble home by Glenade Lake shall shelter us tonight.
Be any doubt to what I write, go visit old Conwell,
And see the grave where sleeps the brave whose epitaph can tell.

*[ ] denotes minor edits from other versions

## AN OTHERWORLDLY STALLION

On a fine spring morning in the year 1700, Padraig Ruadh Meguinney went to his usual place in Glenaniff, in North Leitrim, to find his mare for another day's work. But it turned out to be the last day he would ever farm and no one to this day has been able to explain what happened.

As expected, young Padraig found his white mare grazing on the shores of a little lake on the boundary of Gortenachurry and Carrowrevagh. But he was quite taken aback to see a mighty black stallion standing beside her. He had never seen the horse before or heard anyone talk about its existence – unusual for such a fine specimen of a horse.

On an impulse, Padraig decided to take the big black horse to do his work on the farm that day and give his white mare a well-deserved rest. He led the creature back to his farm and at the end of the day's labour he left home in the evening to return the black horse to the lake shore.

But Padraig did not return home that night and next day the alarm was raised. Neighbours went to look for him, eventually finding his mangled body lying in the waters of the lochaun.

The black horse that 'shone like a crow' was never seen again and the lake was known from that time as Loch Phadraig Rua (Padraig's Red Lake).

## A FEAST IN A GRAVEYARD

When a new graveyard was made in Rossinver, relatives were distressed to discover that the graves of their newly buried kindred were disturbed during the night. When it continued to occur for several weeks, locals set up a watch to find out what was causing the damage.

To their horror, they saw a strange creature emerge at midnight from the deep waters of Loch Melvin and enter the graveyard, seeking out the new graves. The unknown animal, around 2m long, made for the freshest grave and stuck its head into the ground, digging up the clay.

Men fired shots at the animal but it remained unscathed, so they took hatchets and sharp irons and eventually managed to beat the animal to death.

The next day they returned to the graveyard and buried it. They repaired the damage the creature had caused and from that day on no further disturbance happened at the graveyard.

To this day, some still question if the creature was the same species as the Dobharchú of Glenade Lake.


## The Ollphéist's Journey –
## Or How the River Shannon Came to Be

Leitrim's county town, Carrick-on-Shannon, takes its name from the 360km-long River Shannon. By the time the river reaches the town, though still a young waterway, it has already travelled over 40km of the county's border and passed through mighty Lough Allen in the centre of the county. For centuries it was believed that the Shannon begins its above-ground journey at the Shannon Pot, in County Cavan, emerging from the cavernous depths of Cuilcagh Mountain. However, the information board there now mentions that the latest geological surveys have found feeder streams further back into the underground reaches of what is, above ground, County Fermanagh. But with the Shannon Pot being the first visible contact with the infant river, this new fact may not necessarily influence where the tourists choose to go on their pilgrimages to view the beginnings of this great river.

For the county that carries the early reaches – if not the actual source itself – of the longest river in Ireland, it is not surprising to find a range of stories about how the river was formed and how it got its name.

It is said that a great ollphéist, or serpent, once lived in the Shannon Pot. Hearing from the Druids that St Patrick was on his way to Ireland to banish snakes, the ollphéist roused itself from its ancient slumber in the rocky cavern that had been its home and began to dig and burrow to make its escape from the unwelcome grasp of the saint.

As it explored and bored, the first wide channel was formed, which later became Lough Allen. It continued to gouge its path onwards to where Leitrim village is now located and beyond to Carrick, where the channel widened out. Everywhere it went the land was churned up and cattle and sheep were swallowed to feed

its insatiable appetite, much to the great disgust and dismay of all who lived off the land.

The task was easy enough most of the time, thanks to the softness of the ground, but when the ollphéist reached Jamestown, not far from Carrick, the unyielding rock caused such a detour that the exhausted beast had to circle widely to avoid the deep outcrop, forming a bend so large that it nearly created an island. To this day, when the river levels rise, the 'island' is clearly visible.

And so our escapee continued on its way and new lakes swelled and formed in those early reaches, including Lough Boderg and Lough Forbes.

Our river-gouging pioneer then met a mighty gathering of enchanted eels, which it had to battle with for its survival. Near Athleague, the people had had enough. The loss of so many cattle, sheep and pigs caused such a fury that they made a stand against the beast. They were led by a drunken piper called O'Rourke, whose tunes disturbed the ollphéist so much that it gulped and swallowed the piper quickly, before anyone could save him. But the noise of the pipes continued from inside the creature's belly and so disturbed the animal that after a few days the piper was belched out from the ghastly stomach. It is said he lived to tell the tale, for a few days at least, for the strangest thing happened to the piper.

Drunk again, the piper returned to the place where the ollphéist had been previously, though it was now long on its way and water had already filled the channel of the new river. The piper walked into the river and everyone feared he had drowned until the drone of his playing was heard coming from deep in the water. It is said that one of the enchanted eels had survived and O'Rourke had fallen under its magic. The piper never came back on to dry land but it is said that morning and evening the sound of his playing can be heard at the spot, which, from that day to this, is known as The Piper's Hole.

The ollphéist proceeded on his way to the place that is now Lough Ree, where he was attacked by a tribe of venomous serpents. They fought so fiercely that they made the hard ground soft and the soft ground hard and sent stones and great rocks flying more than half a mile up into the air. Floods of blood were running as plentiful as the water itself and people were certain it must be the end of the world. The battle went on for a month without any signs of victory on one side or the other, and the people of the villages round about were living in fear. Finally, slowly but surely, the ollphéist began to triumph and when most of the serpents were dead the survivors asked the ollphéist for peace. He granted it and there was much rejoicing.

After this battle was over, the ollphéist was exhausted and rested for many weeks. During the space of three months it ate only the dead serpents that it had killed in the battle, much to the relief of farmers who were trying to protect their livestock. But no sooner did it set to work again, ploughing through the land, than it demanded its rations of sheep, cows and pigs. Some say that perhaps the ollphéist saw this as its due wage for making the course for such a powerful and helpful river that would irrigate the land.

On went the ollphéist, down towards the west coast of Ireland and its intended destination at the sea, meeting at Portumna an even greater throng of venomous serpents than at Lough Ree. If hundreds met it the first time, thousands met it there. And if the first was believed to have been a battle, it was only light sport compared to the one that took place here. For weeks the battle was heavy and hard. The ollphéist was pierced by the serpents and there was much tearing and killing. In time the 35km length of another great lough was hewn out of the land, this one taking the name of Dearg, meaning red, for it is said that the water there was red with the blood lost in that battle.

The ollphéist was torn and wounded and had to take another long rest, again eating the dead serpents from the battle there. As soon its wounds were healed and the creature was rested, its relentless pursuit for the safety of the ocean began again.

Soon it came to the place where Limerick stands today and was surprised by a troop of enchanted heroes near the spot where the Treaty Stone stands. The warriors threatened the ollphéist and told it to go no further, but to achieve its hunger for the ocean there was no alternative for it but to face battle for a third time. On this occasion it had to contend with the sharp spears, axes and heavy clubs made by human hands. The warriors finally left the beast for dead, having cut and pierced and hacked it so much they did not believe it would survive. But as soon as the sun went down, it came to its senses again and was a little the worse for that encounter – but it was not finished with the warriors.

The ollphéist found the castle where the warriors were still sleeping. It attacked the place and pulled it apart, killing everyone inside, then it went on its way again; the smell of the sea had already reached its nostrils.

There was no more hindrance of unyielding rock or enchanted eel or venomous serpent and the ollphéist stretched itself fully into the soft earth of what became the 113km-long Shannon estuary, until all that had been carved from the land fully filled with water and merged with the great ocean.

But its troubles were not over and this story's ending is not what you might think. For, as soon as our traveller swam out into the deep, endless ocean, a great whale came upon it and the ollphéist struggled in this fourth – and final – battle for its life. However, it was not the battle which took the last breaths from this well-travelled beast. While it was battling the whale, and nearly beaten, a sea-maiden came to its rescue and together they killed the whale.

The sea-maiden and the ollphéist travelled through the ocean, swimming side by side. As they journeyed south along the coastline, they came upon several boat-loads of fishermen.

By now, the great beast was hungry and immediately swallowed them all, boats and men together. The sea-maiden challenged her new companion about what it had done and the creature responded angrily, attacking her. But she was ready for it and drew out a golden comb with venom in it, thrusting it into the ollphéist's eye and blinding it. The ollphéist begged her then to kill it completely, as it would sooner be dead than blind. So she took her scissors and pierced its stomach and the creature died instantly.

The tide was going out and as the waters drew further and further from the coast the body of this great beast, that had carved the hundreds of kilometres of river basin and estuary, marking out what was to become the most majestic of Irish rivers, was washed up on the sands of the Kerry coast.

People heard quickly about this strange beast washed up from the deep ocean and they gathered from near and far to salvage all that they could. Together they cut up and carved open the ollphéist. Within it they found all the fishermen that it had swallowed, not dead but alive and in a heavy sleep at the bottom of their boats. Every part of the beast was used for something, even its bones, which were made into fine oars by the fishermen of Bantry Bay.

And if this story is not true, then there is no water in the sea and no River Shannon in Ireland.

## Postscript

For all the work of the ollphéist in destroying the venomous serpents and the enchanted eels, perhaps some got away. For into the early years of the twentieth century there were still people in the upper reaches of the River Shannon, at Drumshanbo, who claimed sightings of a serpent at the ford on the townland of Deffier. Being the only available ford for miles, travellers had to make the life-threatening choice of whether to use the ford or not. Local tradition said that it showed itself only every seven years, but no one knew exactly when it would rise up from its slumber. When travellers chose to cross at the wrong time, lives were reported to have been lost.

It is claimed that St Patrick stood with his crosier and chained or settled the serpent so it remained there, which is fine for everyone else living in other parts of the Shannon's course, but not so great for the folk of Drumshanbo.

The local lore passed on from those who witnessed its surfacing claim its body to be twice as thick as the largest oak tree and as black as the ace of spades. When it rose from the river, about half of its body would appear, rearing 15m in the air with its two eyes blazing like creels of turf. The swish of the water as it rose and spun created a wave 500m high on either side of the river and the waters of the river remained muddy for miles afterwards.

Then, once again, the serpent resumed its next seven-year slumber and the people were left to cross the ford in safety.


## How the Shannon got its Name

What do ripe, red rowan berries, hungry salmon, bright, young inquisitive girls and a patriarchal society have in common? Everything when it comes to knowledge!

It would seem that, when some of these rowan berries fell from a particular tree into water, the hungry salmon living there ate them – with magical consequences.

Firstly, and not so magically, their skin became dotted with red spots. This became the way for those seeking them to identify them from all the other salmon. Secondly, and quite magically, the berry-fed salmon carried the supernatural means for people to become very knowledgeable when the salmon flesh was eaten. For this obvious reason alone, the red-spotted salmon of knowledge were much sought-after by men who wanted to become the most learned in the land. The salmon were notoriously difficult to catch and this added to the creatures being sought after as the prize above all prizes. On top of this, it was said that only men might gain this knowledge – it was not for women to seek.

Many men travelled far to find a salmon of knowledge, often spending years in their committed search. Of course, others had only to supervise the cooking of one to gain that knowledge, as with the young Fionn Mac Cumhaill. The boy was in the company of his master, the poet and sage Finn Eces, who had spent seven years in search of such a creature. When he finally caught one, he instructed the young Fionn to guard the fire on which it was cooking. When hot fat from the nicely-roasted salmon burned young Fionn's thumb, the lad automatically stuck his throbbing thumb into his mouth to ease the pain and lo, the knowledge sought for so relentlessly by his master became his in an instant. Finn Eces' hopes were dashed and all the knowledge he sought became young Fionn's.

Now, in the ancient Irish kingdom of Ossory (now mainly in the present counties of Kilkenny and Laois), which is where this particularly important rowan tree was located, there lived a young woman called Sionan who was said to be the granddaughter of Manannaán Mac Lir, the great god of the sea. Sionan had an enormous desire for knowledge and so set out to catch one of these red-spotted salmon, disregarding the fact that only men might gain such a prize.

Her search took her to the well in Ossory, where she succeeded in catching one of the illusive creatures. She already had the fire hot and ready to save time and so she immediately prepared the fish and put it on the hot coals. As soon as it was cooked she put the first morsels in her mouth and was immediately overwhelmed by a surge of water bursting from the land. It swept westwards and carried Sionan with it until she was lost in the great new river, which from then on was named after her.

## REFERENCES

**An Dobharcú:** Joe McGowan, *Echoes of a Savage Land*, Mercier Press, Cork, 2001. ISBN 1 85635 363 X, p380ff.

**An Otherworldly Stallion:** Researched and collected by Patrick Tohall of Knappaghmore, Sligo, in 1944, and included in *Echoes of a Savage Land* by Joe McGowan, p377.

**A Feast in a Graveyard:** A feast in a graveyard – NFCS195:29; Thomas Ferguson (78), Gornaderry, Kiltyclogher. Kiltyclogher (B) School. Teacher: Domhnall Ó Gallchlbhair.

**The Ollpheist's Journey:** main source of whole story: Douglas Hyde, Legends of Saints & Sinners, published by T Fisher Unwin, London, 1915. Accessed online on http://archive.org/stream/legendsofsaintss00hyde#page/258/mode/2up. Fragments of story – NFCS 210:24; Mrs Hunt, Jamestown. Collector: John (her grandson), An Mhainistir, Cara Droma Ruisc. Teacher: an Bráthair Eoghan. NFCS210:154. Collector: John McWeeney, Dromore, Carrick on Shannon. Postcript – NFCS208:149. Corderay School. Teacher: Seán Ó Céilleachair.

**How the Shannon got its Name:** Main source Patrick Kennedy, Legendary Fictions of the Irish Celts, 1866, p284 in original. Irish folklorist, Dublin bookseller, and collector and preserver of the varied tales of County Wexford. As seen on http://www.libraryireland.com/LegendaryFictionsIrishCelts/IV-23-1.php and also here http://www.sacred-texts.com/neu/celt/lfic/index.htm

2

# SMALL MOUNTAINS, TALL TALES

It is jokingly said of County Leitrim that the land there is sold by the gallon, owing to the plentiful supply of lakes and rivers. But Leitrim is also graced with several notable small mountains and hills, mainly in the north.

The highest point in Leitrim is on Truskmore ('big cod') SE Cairn, at 631m, in the Dartry Mountain Range – although the actual summit of this peculiarly shaped mountain is in County Sligo. Near to Truskmore is Tievebaun ('grassy slope'), the second highest point, at 611m. Sliabh an Iarainn ('mountain of iron'), which rises from the eastern shore of Lough Allen and stands at 585m, is the third highest mountain in Leitrim. It is well-known for its rich mineral resources and was the site of an iron mining works until the late nineteenth century. Long before that, local legend has it that these mines were worked by Gaibhnen, the smith-god of the ancient Tuatha Dé Danann, with whom the nearby village of Glangevlin in County Cavan is associated. Glangevlin – which translates as the Kingdom of the Glan – is traditionally named after the mythical cow, Glas Gaibhleann, which belonged to Gaibhnen. The Gap of Glan was supposedly created by the cow when it ran away from the blacksmith's forge. A more modern interpretation of the name is Glen with the Fork – much less interesting for mythology-hungry tourists, of course.

## THE LORD OF BENBOW

As well as associations with ancient mythical tribes, these mountains have gathered about them wild and far-fetched tall tales, not

the least of which concerns a quirky 'lord' who lived on Benbo ('hill of the cow's horns'), near Manorhamilton. This peculiar character is said to have lived on the mountainside, using the natural environment of rocks and caves for his home. Many versions of his adventures abound in and around the landscape of this part of the county, some in prose and a lovely version as a poem. They variously have the son of this fellow setting off to find his fortune in Scotland … or was it America … or maybe it was England … such is the range of possibilities, depending on the exaggerations of the tale-teller!

The good news is that in whichever land you want to believe that he found his fortune, he was blessed with a wife and lived happily ever after. The secret of his true origins was never revealed to his in-laws, thanks to the help of one of her father's servants who was sent out to do some prenuptial, private detective work. And later, when the new wife begged her husband to show her his homeland, the presence of a few thousand midsummer bonfires, which happened to be blazing brightly when they arrived in Ireland on St John's night, scared her sufficiently (for reasons to be revealed in the poem that follows) and she never discovered the truth about her husband's unusual birthright.

NB: In this poem, the name of the hill is spelled Benbow. Elsewhere, I use the more common spelling of Benbo.

> There was a wee man, just four feet and a half,
> His voice was like silver and merry his laugh.
> He was loved by his neighbours where e'er he did go
> And they gave him the title the Lord of Benbow.
>
> A rock on the mountain by providence designed
> Had served for three walls of his house so sublime.
> He taught a wee school in pull-a-Ding-Dong more
> Just a hole in the ground without carpet or floor.

He was a philanthropist and taught his school free
But many a fat kid and milch goat got he.
So many, indeed, that they formed a guard
To hold up intruders to his castle yard.

His first-born son was a beautiful beau
And over the England this hero did go.
By his learning he rose there to fortune and fame
And soon fell in love with a beautiful dame.

Her father was rich and a lord of the soil
When he heard of their courtship said he with a smile,
''Ere I give my consent I am wishful to know
If this man is a son of the Lord of Benbow.'

Soon a faithful ambassador o'er the channel he sent
But before he departed to our hero he went
To receive the particulars of how he would go
To the home of his father, The Lord of Benbow.

'Old friend,' said the hero, 'you can fix it for me
'by the tidings you bring from far over the sea.'
With a farewell shake hands not so empty says he
'I'll bring him good tidings from over the sea'.

The news that he brought to her father was grand
That at 1,000 feet high his castle did stand,
That through all his estate where e'er he did go
They all loved and revered the Lord of Benbow.

'When I approached his castle so grand,
His bodyguard all to attention did stand,
Each presented two pistols in a fashion so rare,
And ushered me up to the Lord's great chair.

'My host he has told me that no one ever yet
Had counted correctly the number of its feet
He dined at a table a thousand years old
That's supposed to cover vast treasures of gold.

'No money could purchase his precious salt-stand,
It never was modelled by a human hand
His towel was neither too soft nor too hard
Held ready for him by his bodyguard.

'It never was woven nor never was spun
And life through each thread of his towel did run.'
When he finished his story to the great English Lord
With the young couple's wishes he was in concord.

And after the marriage the young bride would go
To see the domain of the Lord of Benbow
So her husband soon planned for the voyage aright
And they landed in Dublin one bonfire night.

With the country ablaze to his young bride says he,
'This conflagaration's for you and for me
We have more than a hundred miles yet to go
And thicker and higher those fires shall grow.

'We'll never be able to stand it,' says he
'Until things settle down we'll go back o'er the sea.'
His terrified bride back to England did go
And she never more sought for the Lord of Benbow.

## An Unusual Way to Come by a Cow … and Name a Mountain

A man who lived on Benbo is perhaps the person whose courage to follow his instincts gave the mountain its name.

For three consecutive nights, this man had the same dream. In the dream he was told that, if he went up the mountain at a certain time, he would see a cow come out of the lake on the mountain top. In order to keep the cow, he would have to stand between the lake and the cow as it ate the grass. Finally, according to the dream, if he was able to spit at the cow three times before she returned to the water, she would be his.

He followed his dream to the letter and he was able to lead the cow from the mountain top lake to his own fields.

Perhaps this is why Benbo means the Hill of the Cow's Horns. Perhaps. Or perhaps because its double peak resembles the horns of a cow. You decide!

## The Twice-Richest Mountain in Ireland?

It is said that Benbo is the twice-richest mountain in Ireland, owing in part to a deep deposit of gold that runs eastwards through it, and also to a great treasure that is hidden within the lake at the top of the mountain. But … it is also said that the lake is enchanted and guarded by a cat, which in turn was left by a giant to look after his treasure. Others say there is an eel there too. Between them, the eel and the cat have prevented anyone being able to discover the lake's secret.

Yet it's not for the want of trying, because over the centuries various people came up with ways to try to locate the lake's bounty. Some men bravely swam right to the depths of the lake and along most of its floor, but couldn't quite get into one corner – so they found nothing.

Other men decided to dig a channel to drain the water and they were certain they would find the hidden treasure that way. But alas, the eel showed up and they were too scared to challenge it.

So, to this day, both the mountain and its lake keep their secret.

## CORMAC RIABHAC – THE 'IRISH SAMSON'

The day that a young Irish lad rescued the horns of a bull, if not the bull itself, was the beginning of a legend in the making.

Cormac Riabhac, or O'Ruinne, lived with his family in the mountains of north Leitrim, on the western shore of Glenade Lake. As a young boy, one of his jobs was to help on the family farm, tending their herd of bullocks. One day, a bullock became stuck on a rocky ledge on the mountain and the father instructed his son to try to rescue the stricken animal. Young Cormac did his best, literally grabbing the bull by the horns as the animal tried to regain its foothold. Unfortunately, the animal plunged down the rocky hillside to its death and the young lad had to return home and report the dreadful news to his father.

Naturally, the farmer was disappointed to lose a valuable young bull and he challenged his son about why he hadn't been able to hold on and keep the animal safe.

Legend has it that the young Cormac replied that he had held on as long as he could, and, to prove it, he brought from behind his back the horns that had separated from the bull when the animal finally fell.

It may seem far-fetched but the tales of Cormac's mighty feats of strength have been held in local oral memory since the mid-1700s, when the beginnings of this story are said to have taken place. From this time on it appears that many challenges were placed before the 'Irish Samson' as a continuous test to prove and even attempt to outwit his strength.

Some of the tales have grown arms and legs in the way that such lore can. He is given credit for fighting off troops of English soldiers, which frequently hassled and intimidated the local Catholic communities. Whether or not there is any truth in that is lost in the mists of time, but it is more than likely that Cormac proved his worth in many difficult feats of strength that helped his neighbours.

One such story tells of how he was hired to carry two huge stones, possibly weighing a ton each, from where they had been quarried at Largy to a new corn-mill on the river Bonet, a distance of about 2km.

Cormac strapped the stones to his back and carried them to the mill, one at a time; his strength was beyond human understanding. When the weighty sacks of grain and meal had to be shifted from the mill to the carts, there was one clear candidate to get the heavy job.

As time passed, people looked for ways to try to see what would be the limits of Cormac's incredible strength. Once, some extra-large sacks were made – so big that the grain was loaded into them whilst the giant sacks were on the carts. Everyone saw it as more of a trick challenge as the sacks were so enormous; no one really expected Cormac even to try. Of course, he tried – and succeeded – baffling even the greatest doubters and cynics who gave up their disbelief when Cormac completed the task.

When stories about Cormac's abilities began to spread around Ireland, people came from time to time to pit their strength against his, but not one succeeded. Cormac Riabhac – the 'Irish Samson' – became a legend in his own lifetime and beyond.


## Sí Beag, Sí Mór

Ireland is scattered with tomb cairns, some huge and quite accessible, others tiny, collapsed, hidden, and even destroyed by well-intentioned amateur archaeology or agricultural advances. All across the land tales abound concerning who might be buried in these. In turn, the landscapes inspire the muse in artist, poet, writer and composer, and more layers of connection become moulded into the place.

And so it is with two small unassuming hills near Keshcarrigan. They carry in their names a special association with Ireland's greatest harper-composer. And, according to some local traditions, the bodies of two of the country's mythological characters are placed within their earthen depths. There is also no shortage of fairy lore around those small hills, not least by their very names. For they are called Sí Beag (Sheebeg) and Sí Mór (Sheemore), meaning 'little mound of the fairy' and 'big mound of the fairy'.

There is always contradiction in mythological tales about place, time and sometimes even ancestry, and so it is with claiming the precise details of one of mythology's most famous love triangles.

Over many, many centuries, the people who have lived around these hills stake a claim that Sí Beag is the burial place of both Fionn Mac Cumhaill, great warrior of the Fianna, and his unrequited love, Gráinne, daughter of High King Cormac Mac Airt. Other versions of this famous tale, however, state that Gráinne is buried with her lover, Diarmud, in Ben Bulben, the base for the Fianna, in neighbouring County Sligo. Diarmud was the handsome young Fianna warrior with whom she eloped at her betrothal feast to the more elderly and less desirable Fionn. Yet another version says that they are buried in a cave above the Gleniff Horseshoe loop, also in County Sligo. Or that Diarmud is there on his own and …

There can be only one burial place, and, for the sake of a good story to tell, Leitrim's version – that the cairn atop the hill of Sí Beag near Keshcarrigan is definitely the place – is as valid as any. Not that modern political intervention can make it any more water-tight, but the association is also now marked by a sculpture depicting the young Fionn with the salmon of knowledge, one of the many aspects by which his character is well-known. It is placed at the bottom of Sí Beag and was unveiled in 2004 by the then President of Ireland, Mary McAleese.

In the 1930s the cairn was excavated and two bodies, believed to be one female and one male, were found. For locals who enjoy their association with the mythical memory, it was confirmation enough that the bodies could be Fionn and Gráinne. The skeletons were laid back inside the tomb cairn and the storytelling will continue in Leitrim, Sligo and anywhere else with a grain of possibility to make its own claim to the oral tradition.

Anyone who has heard of the seventeenth-century maestro of the harp, Turlough O'Carolan, will know that he composed a tune by that name. It was no ordinary tune, for it was the first one that he created. Until this point the young harper's giftedness in composition was still unknown. The story by which the immortalised tune came into being is that the harper was staying at the house of a local landowner, Squire Reynolds, at Lough Scur. Squire Reynolds – a harper himself and also a poet – wasn't too impressed with O'Carolan's musical talent and asked him if he composed. When the young visitor announced that he didn't, a challenge was set before him that he investigate the local legend about the two hills.

Squire Reynolds had to go away for a few days and, in his absence, O'Carolan visited the two small hills, where he learned of the lore associated with them and dreamed of a battle between the two groups of fairies who inhabited Sí Beag and Sí Mór. When Squire Reynolds returned, O'Carolan played him the piece of music that came from his musings. This became the first of many hundreds of pieces he composed, inspired by both landscape and people, as he travelled throughout Leitrim, Roscommon and Longford, and entertained the great and the good at their big houses.

Turlough O'Carolan was born in 1670 in County Meath, but owing to the religious and political issues of the times his family had to move west, losing all their ancestral lands. They settled near Carrick-on-Shannon and the young O'Carolan found himself receiving encouragement from a wealthy family at Alderford, in County Roscommon, to develop his musical talent. He was already recognised for his proficiency in the harp when a devastating attack of smallpox at the age of twenty-one left him completely blind.

Whatever the sickness brought with it in terms of disability, it did not stop O'Carolan from developing his great skills in composition and playing. He married and settled in Mohill in Leitrim and his house was awash with the comings and goings of fellow harpers and other musicians. With the help of a mounted guide, he rode from place to place and it is said that in every home he visited he left a new song. He had the financial support of several patrons across the counties and, thanks to their investment and his abundant musical inspiration until his death in 1738, he left his imprint in harp music in Ireland. Whether to him directly, or to the great collective heritage and timeless association of the harp with this country, the instrument is symbolised on coins, notes, State letterheads and across the arts and international cultural promotion.

And remember: this great composing talent was brought to light with a little bit of help from a fairy story about two small Leitrim hills called Sí Beag and Sí Mór! Next time you need some creative inspiration, you know where to go …

## REFERENCES

**The Lord of Benbow:** With permission from UCD to use in full. NFCS 200:148-151; Mrs Lynch, Bohey. Collector: Lizzie Lynch, Cill Chuisigh School. Teacher: P Ó Damhnaigh. Some adjustments made to this from the version in NFCS201:3-9; Mrs O Neill, Kilcossey, Dromahair. Collector: John O Neill, Kilcossey School.
**An Unusual Way to Come by a Cow:** NFCS195:289. Collector Thomas McTernan, An Cluainín Í Ruairc school. Teacher: Aodh Ó Floinn.
**The Twice-Richest Mountain in Ireland:** NFCS196:56, 58; Cluainín Uí Ruairc (C). Teacher: Charlotte G Dillon.
**Cormac Riabhac, the Irish 'Samson':** *Leitrim Guardian* 1982. Also – NFCS189; Pat McNulty, Farmer, 85, Carnduff, Glenade. Gleann Éada School. Teacher: Bean Uí Mhaolaith.
**Sí Beag, Sí Mór:** various sources.

# 3

# LOST TO
# THE FAIRY AND
# FOUND AGAIN

Back in the days when the folk imagination centred around a deep connection to otherworldly explanations for strange events, the blame for unnaturally disturbed or deformed babies and children was placed squarely in the hands of fairies. They had every trick in the book when it came to taking healthy and happy beloved babies and children from their cradles and beds and replacing them with 'changelings' – children not born naturally into a human family. Amidst the resulting anguish and grief to the human families, they desperately needed to find a way to retrieve their true children. Often, the solution lay with finding a wise woman who would prescribe a range of peculiar instructions involving red-hot pokers, boiled eggshells, herbal soups and other strange concoctions. And there was always the risk that the assumed offending child might not be a changeling in the cradle, just a grumpy baby. It took more than courage to thrust a red-hot poker down a baby's throat.

Leitrim has its own share of tales about changelings and fairy kidnappings, even of brand new brides and mothers being stolen. Some were returned. The first two stories in this section, about a changeling baby and a young girl, are reprinted here in full in the form in which they were recorded in the school's collection. The several smaller stories following these are retellings.

## THE EGGSHELL BREW THAT UNHINGED AN IMPOSTER

*I love this tale for the clear sound of the spoken voice coming through – it feels like the narrator is sitting in the same room, telling it now.*

There wasn't a better doing man in all Leitrim or the next county to it than Billy Brogan. He had a tidy farm, laid out in nice square little fields and the crops o' spuds he used to have, it was before forty-six, used to be the wonder of the whole parish.

His wife was as thrifty as himself, a brave and smart wee woman that was always sure to have the hens layin' in the right time an' everything in its own place.

But for all that, things can't run smooth the whole time and trouble came to the Brogans an' I'll just tell ye now.

There was a big family in it, all fine childer, but the youngest, a wee boy of about a year old, was the healthiest specimen of a babby every you beamed an eye on, blue eyed and flaxy haired, an' him with skin like a lily an' there wouldn't be a whimper out of him from June to January an' from January back to June.

Well, the whole family was pettin' him an' admirin' him when what happened but didn't he take sick one evenin' at the dusk, an' the howlin' he made all thro' the night was something terrific, and the next mornin' nobody that ever saw him would believe it was the same child.

He was shrivelled up into half his size an' him squallin' an' cryin' an' puttin' faces on him that would make ye shiver in your shoes, an' as day followed day 'twas worse he was gettin' an' his poor mother that miserable an' put about that if your heart was made of marble you'd have a pity for her.

Now the fairies were very plentiful at this time an' there was an' ould fort not a stone's throw from the Brogans' house, an' I used to hear my grandmother, God be good to her, sayin' that many a time she listened at night to laughin' an' the grandest music comin' out of it an' hundreds of wee lights runnin' round it.

So it was no wonder that the ould people of the district would say that Brogan's youngest child had been exchanged by the 'wee folk' an' the dawny craythur left in its place.

What could poor Mrs Brogan do but believe what everyone was tellin' her but, for all that, she didn't care about hurtin' the 'thing', whatever it was, for although its face was as withered as an old man's of eighty, an' its body a mere bag of bones, still it was very like her own child in its features, an' she couldn't somehow find it in her heart to roast it alive or burn off its nose with a red-hot poker, although these remedies were often suggested to her for the gettin' back of her own child.

Now at this time there lived up at the back of Benbo Mountain, in a wee mud-wall cabin, a very wise woman known locally as Sorcha Ruadh.

She was a quare ould damsel an' the people were afeard of her, though she had charms for curin' warts an' cancers an' colics, an' I couldn't tell you what all, but it was supposed that Sorcha used to have dalins with a black gintleman that I hope none of us will ever meet, an' it was said that she could turn herself into a hare quicker than you'd take off your hat.

Be that as it may, didn't Moll Brogan walk the ten long miles across the mountain to get the advice of Sorcha about the changelin' an' as soon as she stepped in the wee cabin didn't the ould hag, squattin' in the chimney corner, say to her, 'You're in trouble this mornin', Moll Brogan.'

''Tis well you may say that, Sorcha Ruadh,' says Moll, 'an' good cause I have to be in trouble for there was my wee Mickeen, as fine a baby as ever was seen, taken out of his cradle without as much as a by your lave, an' a miserable rawny of a shrivelled up leprechaun left in his stead. It's no wonder the sarra would be on me, Sorcha Ruadh.'

'Small blame to you, Moll,' says the ould lassy, 'but are ye dead certain about it bein' a leprechaun?'

'Could I be certainer, Sorcha,' says Moll. 'Haven't I me own two eyes an' didn't Nancy Reilly know what it was at once, an' isn't she the ouldest an' wisest woman in our county?'

Sorcha said nothing for a few minutes an' she turned a look on poor Moll thant was like to freeze the heart in her, so wild an' quare it was, an' after a while says she, 'Will you take an' ould woman's advice, Moll Brogan, though you'll maybe be sayin' to yourself 'tis foolish?'

'Sorcha Ruadh,' says Moll, pluckin' up courage, 'will ye say can yet get me my own child back?'

'Do as I'm goin' to tell ye,' says the ould wan, 'an' you'll soon know an' here's what you've got to do.

'Take the big pot that ye boil the pigs' feedin' in an' fill it full of water on top of the biggest fire that ever blazed on your hearth an' lave it there till it's frothin' over like mad.

'Then you'll go an' get nine new-laid blue duck eggs, an' break them an' be sure ye keep the shells but fling away the rest.

'When that's finished put the shells into the boilin' pot an' you'll soon know wheather it's your own gossoon or not.

'If you find out that it's not a right thing in the cradle, redden the poker in the fire an' drive it down his throat, an' I'll go bail he won't give you much bother.'

Moll started back for home an' done what ould Sorcha tole her.

She put on a reekin' fire of turf that would dry a crop of oats, an' soon had the big pot boilin' at a rate that never was seen afore.

The bucko in the cradle was lyin' quiet without a chirp out of him but now an' again he'd turn an eye after Moll an' a cold stitther in it that would wean a foal, an' he into watchin' the big fire an' the big pot an' didn't he sit up straight when he saw the egg shells goin' in an' says he, in a cracked voice like a very ould man's, 'What is that you're doin' Moll Brogan?'

Poor Moll nearly fell out of her stannin' with fright when she heard the child of a year ould talkin' but she contrived to keep her wits together until she got the poker rammed into the heart of the fire, sayin' to the playboy, 'It's brewing I am avick.'

'An' what might ye be brewin' Moll Brogan?' says the quare thing, an' Moll says to herself, 'I wish the poker was red,' but out aloud says she, 'Is it what I'm brewin' you want to know avick? Well it's eggshells Awomy,' says she.

With that, up jumps the playboy again an' him gigglin' fit to split his sides, an' says he, 'I'm above a thousand years in the world an' I never seen eggshells brewed before.'

By this time the poker was mad red an' without more ado Moll seized it an' made for the cradle an' crammed it into the open mouth of the thing that was grinnin' at her.

It let one screech that the like of it never was heard an' Moll fell down in a dead faint.

When she came to her senses again the first thing she saw was the poker stannin' in a tyub of cold water at the other end of the kitchen an' when she took courage to look into the cradle, what does she see lyin' there sleepin' as sound as a top? Only her own babby as fresh an' fair as ever he was.

An' to end my story, let me tell you, that child grew up to be one of the strongest men that ever was reared in Leitrim an' only died a few years ago an' him nearly a hundred years ould.


## FAIRY FINGERS POINT TO THE TRUTH

*As with the previous story, this one is used with permission from UCD.*

About eighty-five years ago [the mid-1800s], in the townland of Killinagarnis, Annie Flynn, a child of about ten years, was sent on a message to a house named Boles on a fine summer's evening after sunset. She did the message and returned home looking all right but the next day she became ill and lay on a couch in the mud cabin.

Her father and mother did all in their power to nourish and restore her to health, but day by day she sank lower and got weaker until at the end of a few years she became as small as an infant.

She was also cross and very troublesome, insulting every person who spoke to her. On some occasions when neighbours asked for her, she would answer in a little voice, 'Go home and mind your children,' or 'Go home and mind your cattle'. In every case these people found sickness in their families and cattle dying in large numbers.

They were afraid to speak Annie Flynn's name although she was constantly in their minds, for a strange enchantment hung over the district.

After seven years of gloom, her sister Mary met an old woman called Annie Kaine. They discussed her sister's illness, the strange and troublesome way she was and the awful things the people were saying about her.

When Annie heard this, she advised Mary to pull fairy fingers [foxgloves] and boil them without telling any person what they were, then give them to her sister. If she refused to take them, she was an elf but if she took them, she was the true Annie Flynn.

Mary pulled the fairy fingers and left them outside the house. When Annie was asleep she brought out a saucepan, placed the fairy fingers in it and put the lid on tightly. She put the pan on the fire.

Annie was still asleep but when they began to boil she jumped up, although she had not risen for seven years, and in a rage shouted, '*Maunweeu Salough*, what have you in the saucepan? It was that woman Annie Kaine that told you to do it. I won't take them. Drink them yourself.'

The people in the house were now alarmed. They sent for the priest who came at once and questioned her but she gave no satisfactory answers. After a while he threatened her and she finally said she was not the real Annie Flynn but an elf that was left in her place and that after a few days she would make arrangements to go to her own people and for the real Annie Flynn to return. After the priest left the house, the terrible fear left the district and neighbours who did not visit the house for years came – though they stood outside as none had the courage to go in.

In the space of a few hours there were over 200 people standing, some as far as several fields away. At length, some entered. The elf imposter was talking about where the fairies had their fairs and best castles.

On the fifth day, according to arrangements, the elf imposter was taken to Sandy's Alp and a lit candle was placed in her hand. She asked her bearers to go a distance from her. After a while they saw the candle flame circling around and finally it burned out.

When they went back over to the same place, they found the real Annie Flynn, just the same as she was on the night she went on the errand. After they took her home, she remembered nothing, only that she had been sent out with a message and she was at a dance.

Annie Flynn emigrated to America and married a rich man. She had children, grandchildren and great-grandchildren. She is now 105 years old [when this story was recorded] and looks like a woman of 50 years. She attributes her long life and good health to the long sleep she had in Andy Boles' Alp.

## MIDNIGHT BABY FLUSTERS THE COCKS AND HENS

When Paddy Clancy made his entry into the world at midnight up on Benbo Mountain, it was too much for the cock and hens in the barn. Not only did the cock crow thirteen times but the hens began to fly frantically all around the barn and one hen got out from under the door. It too crowed thirteen times – not at all a usual thing for a hen to do.

Such strange happenings didn't auger well and the nurse minding Paddy's mother told Paddy's father to go out and twist the neck of the crowing cock and throw it across the house.

As he stepped out in the dark night and made his way to the barn, he was surrounded by a group of fairies dressed in red. They took him away to a fort but he was able to get away. As he hurried back to the house, he tripped and sprained his ankle. The newborn's father never recovered the strength of his leg and was lame to the end of his days.

Some say that the fairies' intention that night had been to carry off the newborn infant and its mother, but the crowing of the

cocks and hens foiled their plans. All the same, as well as Paddy's father's life-long disability, the child was always delicate and folk say it was on account of the *mí-ádh** left on him by the fairies.

*mí-ádh* – misfortune, ill luck

## THE STRAW WINDOWS THAT SAVED A CHILD

A farmer who lived on the townland of Gowlaun was out visiting his mother one evening not long after the birth of his first child. Now this farmer was so poor that he had straw spread out on the ground around his house and the window cases were filled with heaps of straw called *sliseógs*.

When he was coming back along the path to his house, he noticed that a *sliseóg* was gone from one of his windows. He went over and a voice from inside whispered '*seo*', which means 'here, take it'.

The next thing, he was handed an infant – his own! He suspected he had foiled a fairy plot so he immediately spat on the baby and took it straight away to his mother's house for safety.

When the farmer returned to his own home he went to bed without disturbing his wife, but when they awoke in the morning the infant lying beside them was dead. The mother was distraught and no amount of explaining or consoling by her husband could change her mind; she was convinced her child had perished in the night.

A burial was arranged for the child and all the neighbours gathered in the house to support the grieving parents.

However, they were alarmed when the farmer started throwing heaps of straw on to the fire. They asked him to stop, fearful that the whole house would go up in flames, but he carried on, saying he would warm up the dead baby before burying it.

Immediately the 'baby' shouted out, 'You won't burn me,' and to everyone's horror it jumped out of its cradle and disappeared.

While people stared in disbelief, the farmer hurried over to his mother's house and collected his healthy child, safe and well. Only then did everyone listen to the man's story of what happened the evening before, and they were all delighted to believe him, including his very relieved wife.

It is said that when the fairies handed out the child they had intended to pass it to one of their own kind, who had been waiting outside the window, but when that fairy heard the human footsteps it disappeared. So it was to the father that the child was given instead.

On account of the father spitting on his own child, which protected it forever, there was no fear that the child would be taken again.

## DEAD WOOD

After a day's work in their potato field, brothers John and William Flynn set off for home, but calamity struck when John slipped and fell into a river. He managed to get out of the water and made it home, but a sickness came over him and he died the next day.

The following morning, standing outside their home, William was surprised by a small man passing the house. The stranger spoke to William and instructed him to stand in exactly the same place at five o'clock that evening, when men on horseback would ride past. The small man told William to have a whip ready and to strike the ninth horse.

William did exactly as he was advised. The horses came past, he counted to the ninth horse and gave it a strong smack with his whip. He was surprised and delighted to see none other than his 'dead' brother standing beside him.

Overjoyed, the two young brothers went into the house and over to the bed – where just moments earlier John's corpse had been lying – only to discover the bed contained nothing but a lump of old wood.

The house that was filled with sadness and mourning became a haven of joy. John went on to live for another thirty years.

## MARRIED … WIDOWED … THEN REUNITED

A story passed on through a family called McTernan, who lived in the townland of Gorglancy in Killenummery parish, tells of the death of a wife within twelve months of their marriage and only a week after the birth of their first child.

A few nights after she was buried, her husband, Owen McTernan, was in bed with the infant beside him. Suddenly, at midnight, he awoke to see the fire in the kitchen flare up and a woman walk into the room. There was no mistaking that this was his wife but how could it be, thought Owen McTernan, as she was dead and buried.

The woman took the baby from the bed and sat down by the fireside to feed it. Afterwards, she put the child back into the bed and went away.

This happened three nights in a row and finally, on the third night, Owen McTernan found the courage to speak to the visitor, whom he was sure was his wife. He pleaded with her to stay.

She told him that she could not and that she had been permitted to return only to feed the child. However, she held out a glimmer of hope for her grieving husband: she told him that she would be passing the following evening at midnight, astride a white horse, on a march from Moher Hill to Blasthill Fort. The night would be bright and clear. As the troop of twenty horses passed through a gap in the fort, her husband's only chance would be to pull her from her horse, which would be the sixth, and not to be afraid of anything he saw or heard.

If he succeeded, she would be with him for life.

Owen McTernan needed all his courage to carry out this feat and he rounded up six men to help him. They strengthened their resolve with a drink of poteen and headed for the gap, waiting for the fairies to pass by.

At length, they saw them coming from Moher Hill. Owen McTernan and his friends counted to the sixth white horse and used all their strength and resolve to catch hold of the woman and pull her from the horse.

Thunder and lightning spread across the sky and deafened them, but the men's courage stayed true. That evening Owen McTernan, his wife and their newborn child were reunited as a family, to great rejoicing in the neighbourhood.

They lived a long and happy life.


## ANOTHER HAPPY ENDING FOR NEWLYWEDS

When the Kelly brothers of Mohercreg heard of the death of their only sister a year after she was married, there was much mourning. Her body was laid out and prepared for the wake and folk gathered from her townland as well as from that of her husband's, a Gallagher from Crummy.

The youngest Kelly brother stayed back at the family home to see to the animals before setting out for the wake. As soon as he was ready to leave, he put a crooked sixpence in his gun and set off. On his way past a fort, he saw four men carrying a coffin. Young Kelly fired his gun in their direction and immediately the four strangers put down the coffin and ran off.

The young lad plucked up the courage to lift the lid of the coffin and there, inside, wrapped in a blanket, was his sister. He lifter her out of the coffin and carried her straight back to the Kelly home. There, he laid her out on the bed, sprinkled holy water all around the house and called to some neighbours to keep watch.

Young Kelly put another crooked sixpence in his gun and set off for a second time.

When he reached his brother-in-law's house, it was jammed full of mourners. He complained that he was feeling the cold and put extra fuel on the fire to make it burn hot and fast. When it was blazing, he went over to the bed where his 'sister' was supposedly lying, took 'her' from the bed and threw the body on to the fire.

Whatever 'it' was went up the chimney with a great roar and people thought the roof itself would pull off.

Straight away young Kelly told them what had happened on his way over and everyone followed him back to his home.

There, waiting for them, was his sister, alive and well. She and her husband returned to their cottage and it is said she lived another thirty years after her strange 'death' experience.


## THE FAIRY BLACKSMITH

The following story is reproduced with permission from the Lilliput Press in Dublin, publishers of *The Face of Time, Leland Lewis Duncan 1862-1923, Photographs of County Leitrim*, a collection of photographs and stories compiled by Liam Kelly.

Duncan was born and lived all his life in England. He was related to the Slackes of Annadale in the parish of Kiltubrid near Lough Scur. The family's connections in the area date back to the 1600s.

In the 1880s, from the age of eighteen, Duncan visited the family several times, developing an increasing fascination for the landscape of Sligo and Leitrim. He went to the homes of local people – the poor, the servants and estate tenants – and listened to their stories. His photographs create an invaluable historical insight and he strengthened his collection with the addition of local folk tales which he gathered on his Irish visits.

This story was told to Duncan by Barney Whelan.

There was a poor man in County Leitrim, and he had a sickly son. His son has been a fine healthy boy until he was about three years of age, when he suddenly got ill and donny and, try as they might, they couldn't discover what was the cause. He remained so for four or five years more, and gave all sorts of annoyance to his poor mother and father, screeching and screaming for a thing to eat at all times.

One day his father went to the forge to get his loy irons [heavy spade] laid with the smith. It happened that the smith did one iron remarkably well, and there was a flaw in the other, but the man never noticed it. When he came home with the irons, 'Daddy,' says the sickly little lad, 'show me them irons.'

'What do you know about irons?' says the father. But the lad persevered to look at them, and to please him, his mother handed them to him. The lad looked at them: 'Daddy,' says he, 'this is a good one, but that one is no good; did he throw those two irons on the ground when he did them?'

'No' says the father; 'he gave me this one in my hand, and he threw the other one on the floor.'

'The one he threw on the floor,' says the little lad, 'is a good one; but the one he gave you in your hand is cracked, and nearly broken; and that's the reason he handed it to you, because he knew it wouldn't sound clear on the floor. Go back with it now, and tell him it's a bad iron, and to make it better for you.'

The father went back again to the smith with the iron and said: 'Why did you give me a broken iron, and didn't do it right for me?'

'Who told you that?' says the smith.

'A small little child I have of my own; and he said that because it was bad you handed it into my hand, and the good one you threw on the floor to me.'

'Who told you that?' says the smith.

'Isn't it the case?' says he.

'Well', says the smith, 'whoever told you that is as good a blacksmith as I am, and if I knew who told you, I would give you five pounds, because it is a league among all blacksmiths.'

Says the man: 'It's a sickly little child of my own.'

'Well, if he is,' says the smith, 'he's as good a blacksmith as me.'

So the man was not thankful to him to say his child would be a fairy.

'Well', says the smith, 'stop here till it bees dark, and surely your wife will begin to scold you for stopping out so late. Tell them you could be home half-an-hour sooner, or an hour, but that you were surprised looking at the fort above the house on fire, and that it's all consumed.'

So he went home: and the wife began: 'What kept you out so late? You have your whole day spent with them two irons now.'

'I could be home sooner,' says he; 'but I was surprised to see the fort on fire, and now it's all consumed. I stood an hour looking at it.'

'My word!' says the lad in the cradle, 'my bellows and tools are all burnt.' And out with him, and he never came back.


## References

**The Eggshell Brew that Unhinged an Imposter:** Used in full with permission from UCD. NFCS200:186-192; Dan Carty, Kilcoosey, Dromahair. Collector John O Neill, Cill Chuisigh School. Teacher: P Ó Damhnaigh.

**Fairy Fingers Point to the Truth:** Used in full with permission from UCD. NFCS202:75-78; Denis McMorrow (65), Killavoggy, Dromahair. Collector: Rose Martha McMorrow, Killavoggy School. Teacher: Seán de Faoite.

**Midnight Baby Flusters the Cocks and Hens:** NFCS200:215; Patrick Gilmartin, Bohey, Dromahair. Collector: Margaret Gilmartin, Cill Chuisigh School. Teacher: P Ó Damhnaigh.

**The Straw Windows that Saved a Child:** NFCS202:210; Mary Flynn (80), Tawnylea, Carrick on Shannon. Craoibh Liath school. Teacher: Mrs Doyle.

**Dead Wood:** NFCS207:522; Andrew Redican (70), Crummy, Aghacashal. Collector: Francis Moran, Cormongan school. Teacher: Seán MacAmhalghaidh.

**Married ... Widowed ... then Reunited:** NFCS207:187; Terence McTernan, 54, Corglancy, Dromahair. Collector: Mary Ellen Mostyn, Tulach na Scríne School. Teacher: Ss Mac Fhlannchaoha.

**Another Happy Ending for Newlyweds:** NFCS207:520; Thomas Dalton, Drumhall, Drumshanbo. Cormongan school. Teacher: Seán MacAmhalghaidh.

**The Fairy Blacksmith:** Retold in full with permission from Lilliput Press. *The Face of Time: Leland Lewis Duncan 1862-1923*, by Liam Kelly. Lilliput Press, Dublin 7, 1995, p67

*Further reading suggestions about changelings:*
www.pitt.edu/~dash/ashliman.html
www.pitt.edu/~dash/changeling.html
www.pitt.edu/~dash/folktexts.html
www.pitt.edu/~dash/ireland.html

# 4

# SAINTLY STORIES OF DEEDS GOOD AND NOT SO GOOD

Leitrim's landscape is dotted with physical evidence of pre-Christian and Christian activity, including wells, stone monuments and carvings, and remnants of monasteries and sites of worship.

Stories of mythical characters, holy men and women and Christian saints all interweave with the places that are claimed to be associated with them. Until religious life became more structured in Ireland and written histories began to emerge, the earliest Christian endeavours and the rituals associated with pre-Christian religious practice were transmitted orally. As a result, the line between myth and fact is not always clear, owing to the often exaggerated use of language to describe people, places and events.

This makes historical survey of pre-literate times more of a guessing game than a precise art, although, on the other hand, storytellers are happy with a slice of fact decorated with a helping of fiction, since knowing the absolute 'truth' is less important than the hearing of a good story well told.

In the realm of religious activity, here is one example: much of early Christian proselytising activity in Ireland is laid at the feet of St Patrick, but it is widely accepted by historians that Patrick could not have achieved all that is claimed in his name. It is also accepted that he probably didn't visit all the holy wells which are named after him. Equally, there are many more stories of his wanderings across the land than he realistically could have achieved. The numbers of people he is purported to have converted under his ministry is also said to be exaggerated. Historical study sees all of these claims as an early form of news 'spin', in this case by the church of Armagh, keen to make him their headline man. So there's nothing new under the sun when it comes to propaganda! However, where places, events and people have been woven together to play their part in passing on an explanation for why certain things happened, the drawing in of those colourful threads that are more likely to be fiction can still provide some body to the thinner, paler lines of small fragments of fact.

In the stories that follow I have researched some factual material about the principal saintly figures and settings associated with Leitrim. I have also gleaned some fragments of story lore that will have an element of truth hidden within them but are not to be taken literally. Together they complement each other to provide some understanding of what might have happened.

## St Caillín

One of Leitrim's best known Christian sites is at Fenagh, where St Caillín founded a monastery in the late sixth century. He was born in the first quarter of that century, making him a contemporary of St Columcille (Columba) and of St Ciarán of Clonmacnoise.

Caillín was born in Galway and came from the Conmaicne tribe, who were ousted by the O'Connors. As a result, they divided into several groups, one of which, the Conmaicne Magh Rein, moved to what is now South Leitrim and Longford.

Caillín's father was Niata and his mother was Dediva. He had several siblings and half-siblings, most of whom are recorded as saints and one became a chief Ollam (bard). A short diversion via

Caillín's mother's ancestral line brings in a link to the early work of St Patrick in Ireland.

Patrick's maternal great-grandfather, Dubhthach, was a celebrated Druid and chief Ollam of Ireland in the fifth century. Lóegaire mac Néill, High King of Ireland, was jealous of Patrick's power and gave orders that when he next presented himself at Tara, no one should rise from his seat to do him honour. The next day was Easter day, and it was also a great feast with Lóegaire and his court.

In the midst of their festivity, Patrick visited with five of his companions. No one rose up at his approach except Dubhthach. Patrick blessed Dubhthach, who was the first to believe in God that day. He was baptised and confirmed and he dedicated his life and poetic gifts to Christianity. Dubhthach's nephew, Fiacc, an apprentice to the great bard and a convert and devotee to Christianity, was also present. Both Fiacc and Dubhthach became lifelong friends with Patrick, and Fiacc became the Chief Bishop of Leinster.

As an endnote to this part of the story, there are conflicting versions about whether or not Lóegaire converted to the faith. Amongst several of the early accounts of the life of Patrick, contradictory claims are made that Lóegaire either reluctantly accepted the faith after he and others made several unsuccessful attempts on Patrick's life, or that he refused and stated that he would be buried in the walls of Tara, as his father Niall had wished. There is more concurrence in stories that claim two of his daughters converted.

Now, back to the story of Caillín. The ancient Book of Fenagh speaks of the life and deeds of Caillín. When he began to build the monastery at Fenagh, he faced resistance from the old orders of pre-Christian traditions. Fergal, son of Fergus, King of Breifne, sent the Druids against Caillín and it is said that Caillín turned the Druids into stones, which alludes to the local townland name of Longstone. These standing stones are still visible.

Among the most celebrated stories connected with the life of Caillín concerns the recovery of the lost heroic tale, the Táin

Bó Chúailgne, which had vanished almost completely from the memory of the Filí (storytellers/poets) of Ireland. Some of them knew one part and some another, whilst the complete story was lost.

The story goes that Caillín was approached by the King of Connacht to see if he could do anything to recover the full epic tale. Caillin invited Columba, Ciarán of Clonmacnoise, Brendan of Birr, and Brendan son of Finnlogh, to meet him at the grave of the great hero of the Táin Bó Cúailgne, Fergus mac Róich. There they fasted and prayed for three days and three nights, requesting that Fergus appear to them – Fergus just happened to have been dead for 500 years! Their request was granted; the ancient hero appeared and he related the whole story of the Táin. It was taken down by Ciarán and Caillín and thus it is claimed that this is how the celebrated epic was preserved. The Táin Bó Cúailgne was one of many accounts found in the book of the Dun Cow, a parchment believed to have been made from the hide of Ciarán's favourite cow. The leather must have lasted well – no less than 600 years – since much of the writing in this manuscript has been dated to the twelfth century and is, so far, the oldest extant manuscript in Irish.

Before Caillín arrived at Fenagh, he had spent quite a bit of time studying. His first tutor was Fintan. He went on to study in Rome and for this journey it is said Fintan gave him 300 ounces of gold. At the end of a long period in Rome, messengers from the Conmaicne were sent to ask Caillín to return and save them. It is claimed he brought with him relics of the twelve apostles and the neck-cloth of the infant Jesus.

The chosen site for the Abbey at Fenagh came in an angelic visitation to Caillín. The angel did not let him rest until he arrived at Fenagh. The monastery at Fenagh was celebrated for its divinity school, at which students from all over Ireland and Europe came to study. The importance of the monastery may be measured by the claims that many of Ireland's kings are buried there. Caillín's remains are in a vault attached to the wall of the Abbey.

## St Máedóc

There are many accounts about slabs of stone which miraculously carried coffins to burial grounds on islands in the middle of lakes. One such slab is also associated with the baptism of a child who was already hailed as 'chosen' prior to his birth. This child, Máedóc (Mogue), also known as Áedan, was destined not only to become one of the key figures in the next generation of Christian leadership but also experienced his first rite of passage from the ministry of Caillín.

Máedóc was born around AD 550 on an island called Inis Breachmhaigh (Inisbrefny) in Templeport Lake, in the present county of Cavan. In those days, the area was known as Magh Slécht. His father, Setna, was a Connacht chieftain of a branch of the Airgíalla called the Fir Lurg, who were in the process of spreading southwards into what is now the counties of Fermanagh and Cavan. His mother, Eithne, belonged to the Ui Fhiachrach, with the result that Máedóc had noble blood through both his ancestral lines.

Máedóc is often referred to as 'Son of the Star' because of a vision his parents had before he was born. One night, while they were asleep, they experienced the vision of a star descending from the heavens and falling on them, heralding the future greatness and sanctity of their yet unborn child. The following day, a report of this miraculous vision spread and many wise people predicated that, since a star had led the Magi to the Christ child, similarly this sign had been given to show that a son would be born, full of the Holy Spirit. Shortly afterwards, while travelling in a chariot, Eithne was met by a Magus (magician) who told his companions: 'This chariot runs under a King.' When he reached the chariot, he said to Eithne: 'Woman, thou hast conceived a wonderful son, and he shall be full of God's grace.'

One summer morning, Caillín found the ground unseasonably covered with snow and his cattle had stampeded during the night.

Tracking their hoof-prints in the snow, he found them on the shore of Inis Breachmhaigh, gazing towards the island, where a weaver and his wife lived. In answer to the saint's inquiries, the weaver's wife informed him that a strange woman had asked for shelter the evening before and during the night she had given birth to a son, and that a hazel distaff which she had held in her hand had burst into blossom. The weaver had taken his boat with him to look after his nets on the lake and there was no means of sending the infant over for baptism. Urged by Caillín, the weaver's wife looked for something flat on which to float the child over to the mainland. All she could find was an enormous flagstone, which formed the hearthstone in her cottage, but, of course, she couldn't move it. Caillín told her to place the child on it and, as soon as she did so, the stone moved to her touch and the infant was miraculously wafted to the other side of the lake. Having been baptised by Caillín, the infant was sent back in the same miraculous manner. On the flagstone was a bell – forever since known as Mogue's Bell – which was venerated in the island church for centuries afterwards. The holy water font in St Mogue's church in Bawnboy, County Cavan, is said to be made from part of that stone.

Máedóc studied at Finnian's school at Clonard Abbey. Even in his early years the fame of his sanctity was widespread and, when disciples began to seek him out, he left Ireland and went to Kilmuine, in Wales, where he became a pupil of St David. He is named as one of St David's three most faithful disciples.

After many years in Wales he returned to Ireland in AD 580, bringing a band of followers, and they settled in Leinster. He founded several monasteries there and in AD 598 the King of Leinster, Brandub mac Echach, convened a synod which agreed that Ferns be made an episcopal see with Máedóc as the first bishop. He was also given a title of Ard-Escop, or Chief Bishop, over the other Leinster bishops.

Máedóc founded thirty churches and a number of monasteries, the first monastery being on the island of Inis Breachmhaigh where he was born.

The monastery he founded at Rossinver on the shores of Lough Melvin is also where he died on 31 January AD 632. He was buried inside the church and a bronze reliquary containing his relics is preserved in Dublin.

## A RARE TROUT: THE GIOLLA RUADH

To this day, the peculiar presence of a type of trout that can be found only in one lough in Ireland is attributed to a miracle by St Máedóc, which took place in the days when the Christian leader lived at the monastery at Rossinver.

The story goes that Máedóc was on his way back to the monastery from nearby Kinlough when he felt hungry. He stopped at a house and asked for something to eat. The woman there, forgetting that it was a Friday, gave the monk cooked chicken. She was horrified when she remembered the day of the week and asked Máedóc for his forgiveness for her dreadful mistake.

He asked her what she would normally eat on Fridays and she replied 'slim cake', because there were no fish in the lough nearby. Máedóc raised his hands in prayer over the remains of the chicken, gathered the bones together and took them down to the lough. He threw them in and a miracle took place. The chicken-that-was became a trout, known since that day as the giolla ruadh (gillaroo), or red servant.

The name of the fish is due to its distinctive colouring – bright, buttery golden in its flanks, with bright crimson and vermilion spots. The giolla ruadh is characterised not only by these deep red spots but also by a chicken-like gizzard, which the fish uses to aid the digestion of hard food items. They feed almost exclusively on bottom-living animals – snails, sedge fly larva and freshwater prawns – except during late summer when they surface to feed.

Some other lakes in Ireland also lay claim to their own unique trout species, created by the miraculous activity of other saints-in-

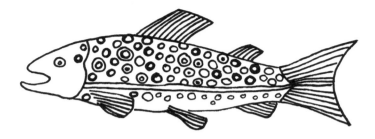

the-making, including Loughs Neagh, Conn, Mask and Corrib. However, it is believed that the unique gene found in the Lough Melvin trout has not been found in the many known trout populations in Ireland and Britain. It is therefore now recognised by its own, original scientific name.

## AN UNHOLY LOOK

A Leitrim chieftain's daughter who lived near Mullies, in the north of the county, was preparing herself for marriage, and she decided to go to Lough Derg on a pilgrimage before her wedding. Her route took her past the monastery at Rossinver, which was established by Máedóc and had a great reputation for its learned inhabitants. However, as she passed by, she was seen by a monk who found her beauty to be so enchanting that he was smitten beyond reason. He decided to keep a watchful eye for her return.

When she passed the monastery on her homeward journey, ready now in mind, body and spirit for her marriage to the son of the chieftain Farrell from Killargue, the unholy monk ambushed and seduced her on the road at a place since named Cornavannoge, 'the cairn of the young woman', or 'the crime of the young woman'.

The shocking incident was more than she could bear. Her purity defiled and her marriage prospects damaged beyond repair, the bride-to-be chose not to return to her family and the sorrow of the wedding that could no longer take place. Instead, she took her own life.

Worried that the chieftain's daughter seemed to be taking longer than expected to return, her husband-to-be set out in search of her, hoping to meet her on her way home.

On the road near Manorhamilton he unexpectedly met a monk who warned him not to continue on his journey, otherwise he would risk the loss of two lives: his and another man's. The chieftain's son was alarmed by this warning but did not heed it, as it made him all the more impatient to find his beloved. He continued on his way in his now desperate quest to find the girl he planned to marry.

Eventually, Farrell's son met the monk who had caused such a dreadful tragedy and found out all that had taken place. It was too much to bear. In the love-torn tussle that followed, he killed the monk. And now the young chieftain's son, who had lost all that he had hoped to live for, fulfilled the prophetic statement made by the first monk he had met on the way – he took his own life.

As a result of the wayward monk's unholy look, three deaths had occurred, two beloved people had not returned home and their joining of the families through marriage was lost for ever.

When the chieftain Farrell found out what had happened to his son and future daughter-in-law, he went to where the sorry business had taken place and buried his son there. Since that time, the area is known as Kilmacurril, which means wood or church of the son of Farrell.

## ST FRAOCH

A hardy warlike tribe, the Con Maicne, inhabited what is now the parish of Cloone in south Leitrim. It is likely that the tribe moved into the area during the first and second centuries, dislodging the previous settlers. Mythology points to a story that

Conn, son of Maeve, Queen of Connacht, suffered from some form of foot disability. Maeve preferred to have strong, fit men around her so she banished the unfortunate son to Cluain, where he founded his own dynasty.

The Con Maicne survived well into the sixth century, still retaining their warlike attributes and defying the best of Christian proselytising that passed through their land. However, eventually one of their number, a young prince called Fraoch, converted to Christianity and founded a monastery in the area, then known as Cluain Con Maicne, the 'fertile meadow of the Con Maicne'.

One account of Fraoch's conversion suggests he came to faith through Patrick, but the dates don't add up as Patrick died in 461 and Fraoch in 570. This calls into question the origin of a well-documented bell, which Patrick is reputed to have left Fraoch. The story goes that the bell became known as Clog na Fola, the Bell of Blood. Its custodians used it for measuring gold, corn and other commodities, but they were said to have removed the tongue of the bell and kept for themselves the extra gold which the bell then held. When Fraoch discovered this dishonesty, it is said he cursed the cheats and said they would always be poor. He also prophesied that the desecrated bell would be the cause of much discord and bloodshed. In later years the bell was used cunningly to test the truthfulness of witnesses in court trials and was supposed to ring if a witness told a lie, even though it had no tongue. However, it was used to convict innocent people and it became a cause of discord and trouble among the tribe. So great a nuisance had it become that a travelling friar was supposed to have buried it secretly somewhere in Aughavas. So Clog na Fola fulfilled Fraoch's prophecy.

Difficult as the Con Maicne tribe were to evangelise, they clung to their new-found faith once they converted. It is believed that Columba visited Fraoch at the monastery in Cluain, as well as the neighbouring monastery of Caillín at Fenagh after the Battle of Cul Dreimhne (also known as the Battle of the Book). He sought advice from his wise teachers and both are believed to have advised him to take his punishment of self-imposed exile. Columba was one of many holy men said to have visited Cluain, as Fraoch was renowned for his wisdom and piety.

Fraoch died around 570 and his feast day is celebrated on 20 December. The work at the monastery continued under the leadership of his nephew, Berach, or Barry, who was born in the townland of Gortnalougher, just outside Cluain. The story of Berach's birth is told that, one night, as Fraoch stood outside his rough stone cell in Drumharkin Glebe, he saw a brilliant light over his sister's house in Gortnalougher. He told his attendants to go to that house where they would find a newborn baby boy and to bring the baby to him immediately. It is said that he reared the young Berach on goat's milk and foretold that he would be the God-sent saviour of his tribe. Fraoch taught him at the monastery in Cluain and Berach later became a disciple of Cóemgen or Kevin of Glendalough, before establishing a monastic settlement at Killbarry in County Roscommon. Berach died in AD 595.

Berach's sister, Midabaria, was abbess of a convent at Bumlin, the present parish of Strokestown, and another relative, Raoiriú, founded Teampall Raoileann on the east bank of the River Suck in the parish of Creagh, near Ballinasloe, County Galway. Raoiriú was one of the first missionaries amongst the eastern Uí Maine, one of the oldest and largest kingdoms of Connacht. In the sixth century, Cairbre Crom, king of the Uí Maine, gave Teampall Raoileann to the monastery at Clonmacnoise.

There is a record of a battle being fought somewhere in the area of Cluain between the O'Connor and Reynolds clans in 1251, and that by that stage a large part of Cluain had ceased to be a monastic settlement. However, as late as 1519 there are records showing that the coarb, or presbyter, of Cluain Con Maicne died. Coarbs of Cluain, from 1400 up to the time of the Reformation, would all appear to have the same name, Mc Thedheadain, modernised Keegan.

In 1522 Pope Adrian II conferred the rectory of Cluain on a canon of Ardagh, Aodh Mac Conmidhe. In the following century Bernard Duignan was pastor of Cluain. He was one of the learned family, the O'Duignans of Castlefore.

In recent years, refurbishment and development at the graveyard which surrounds the site of the old monastic settlement found that a high cross once stood there. Various cross fragments and sculpted figures with a substantial cross base, known locally as the wart well, were unearthed.

## A TASTE OF HIS OWN MEDICINE

When St Patrick was building a wall around a graveyard at Glenade, he ran short of money and asked a local man for help. The man had no money to give him but offered his bull to Patrick, hoping that the bull would attack and kill him.

Since Patrick's men were hungry from their work, the bull was killed and provided much-needed sustenance for the monks.

The bull's owner was furious that the bull did not kill Patrick and demanded that his animal be returned. Of course, there was nothing left of it but skin and bone, but Patrick placed the skin on the bones, prayed over the dead creature's remains and suddenly the bull assumed its own shape again.

Pleased with himself, the farmer walked back towards his own place, followed by the bull. As the farmer reached his land, the bull attacked and killed him then disappeared into the air without trace.

## SALMON SCARCE AND SALMON A-PLENTY

There are two short rivers which border the tiny stretch of land forming Leitrim's coastline. The River Drowes, to the north-east, is on the county boundary with Donegal and the River Duff, to the south-west, is on the Sligo county boundary. Both rivers are famed for their salmon fishing, with the Drowes often bringing in the first salmon of the season on opening day, 1 January.

A story is told that St Patrick was travelling in the area one day. When he reached the River Duff he saw some people fishing and asked them for a salmon. They refused, on the grounds that the salmon were scarce. Patrick is said to have replied that they would be scarcer still.

He went on his way and reached the River Drowes, where some more people were fishing. There he asked a man named Cassidy for a fish and he was given one immediately. As a result it is said that Patrick assured him that there would always be a Cassidy to fish in the river and salmon for them to catch.

# DEAD MAN'S POINT

Long before Christian times, a tiny island at the north end of Lough Allen was used for burials. Some historians suggest the tradition goes back to the time of the Fir Bolg.

The island is called Inismagrath and it is tucked in close to the shore, near the point where the River Shannon enters the lough. A church was founded on the island around 520 by 'lively' Hugh, who is described in the next story. The island became a place of retreat for monks from far and near who were happy to get away from the busyness of their thriving monasteries. In the early Christian period, many faithful asked to be buried on the island, as well as local Christians who favoured their centuries-long tradition of island burials.

The launching point for the journey to the island was known as gob na ndaoine marbh, 'the dead people's point', more commonly referred to as Dead Man's Point. It was the nearest part of the mainland to the island, less than 2km away.

The short journey out to the island to perform the burial was often a challenge because of the strong winds that, to this day, whip up dangerous waves on the lough. Relatives of a bereaved person might end up marooned on the mainland shore minding the coffin, for several days if necessary, until the winds calmed. Sometimes several coffins would line up at the same time, all waiting for their opportunity to be taken to the island.

Long before boats were used to convey the coffins on the journey, tradition has it that a large stone flag was used to float the dead to their final resting place. A prophecy claimed that if anyone who was not religious was placed on the flagstone, there would be no more burials on the island. The story goes that, when some outsiders put this to the test one day, the flagstone broke in two and sank to the bottom of the lake. One part of the flag was later washed up at Dead Man's Point.

In the mid-1700s Lady Townsend gave permission to Fr Myles McPartlan to build a church on the eastern shore of the lough in an attempt to encourage local people to stop making the risky trip to the island. A strange condition of the permission was that the building would have no roof. The church was built in the townland of Killadiskert and is now known as Kilbride Church. The date of the construction of the church, carved on the lintel over the doorway, is 1735. The church grounds gradually replaced the precarious journey to the island as the choice of burial place.

## St Hugh – 'Lively Hugh'

A late fifth-century saint, whose ministry around Lough Allen was prolific, earned the name of 'lively Hugh', or Beo-Aoidh. Hugh was the Bishop of Ardcarne, a parish near Boyle in County Roscommon. He is believed to have founded a monastery there early in the sixth century.

Around 500, he founded a school or monastery in the townland of Cleighranbeg in Ballinaglera, on the north-eastern shore of Lough Allen. Tradition has it that many priests were educated and ordained there. Whilst there are no remains of the monastery, its existence is remembered in the name of the parish for which the Irish form, Baile na gCléireach, translates as 'the town of the clergy'.

Tobar Bheo-Aoidh (St Hugh's Holy Well) is also found in Cleighranbeg, and the river which forms the boundary between Cleighranbeg and the neighbouring townland, Cleighranmore, is called Tobar Bheo-Aoidh River. On the shores of Lough Allen, an old graveyard in the townland of Fahy used to be known as Killbeog or Cill Beo-Aoidh (the church of Beo-Aoidh).

In the previous story about Dead Man's Point, the connection with Hugh can be made as the founder of the first Christian Church on Inismagrath, an island in Lough Allen, in 520.

Tradition has it that, before his death, Hugh had a vision or dream telling him when he would die and where he would be buried. One account suggests that Hugh was directed in a dream to walk towards the mountain Sliabh an Iarainn and look in the direction of the lough, where he would see a piece of land covered with snow. He did as directed and that is how the burial place of Fahy was selected. Another story tells that he saw the mountain covered in snow, while a green spot on the edge of the lake was destined to be his last resting place. It is believed that Hugh was buried at Killbeog when he died in 524.

The whereabouts are unknown of the Bell of St Beo-Aoidh, which was passed on to the parish of Ballinaglera, but it is said that many miracles were attributed to its presence.

## REFERENCES

**St Caillín:** various sources, including www.fenagh.com, with permission.

**St Máedóc:** various websites, including Wikipedia.

**A Rare Trout:** NFCS191:85; John Connolly, shanachie, 45, Gurteendarragh, Kinlough. Buckode School. Teacher: Muirs Mac Gearailt.

**An Unholy Look:** NFCS198:304. Broca School. Teachers: T. Ó Chioráin/S. Ó Gallchobhair.

**St Fraoch:** bulk of content based on article on Cloone Parish website with permission from its author, Evelyn Kelly; also background from Michael Whelan's book *The Parish of Aughavas, its History and its People* (1998); internet references.

**A Taste of his Own Medicine:** NFCS189:20; James Liffney, Farmer, 83, Prughlish, Largydonnell. Gleann Éada School. Teacher: Bean Uí Mhaolaith.

**Salmon Scarce and Salmon A-Plenty:** NFCS189; Michael MacTernan sen (77), Glenague, farming.

**Dead Man's Point:** www.dbo.ie/loughallen/index.htm

**St Hugh:** www.sainthughs.com and other internet references.

# 5

# EMERGING FOLK HEROES FROM REAL-LIFE EVENTS

By folk tales, we usually mean old stories that have been passed on orally, often with a strong element of invention, yet also with a ring of truth to them. However, sometimes the line separating what is a 'made up' story and what is a story about something that more than likely happened is hard to place. When studied closely, most things could have taken place, so when is a story only a folk tale? And when is a story not a folk tale?

All of the stories gathered for this collection have a ring of reality to them, especially when the people and places are recognisable, even if not all the contents are verifiable. However, owing to their significance to Leitrim's history, I have used my collector's licence to include some stories about people who lived in Leitrim and the events associated with them. In times to come they may grow arms and legs and slip into the 'did this really happen?' category and move towards the realm of folk tales. As a storyteller, I am happy with that because it keeps them in circulation and adds a dimension to their continued telling and remembering. At the same time, historical study can continue to dig into the past and gather new fragments of information to add to what is already known. I include these pieces as examples of historical people and events worthy of mention in this collection. I am sure that, besides these, there are many other characters waiting in the shadows to tell their stories afresh.

This chapter brings together four people: three from Leitrim and one from Spain. The Leitrim three are: a woman who was the first in America to have a statue raised to her memory; a man who was wrongly hanged but whose last words led to a legacy of an unusual healing charm; and a well-loved poet. Each has been brought back into contemporary awareness through the efforts of individuals and groups who want the lives and achievements of these three people to be heard again and, in the case of the hanged man, for the truth of his plight to be pieced together and retold.

The reader may well ask how a Spaniard fits into a book of Leitrim stories, but the peculiar addition of this character is due to a remarkable story of survival during one of the many complex periods of Irish history. This man was able to write about his experiences and this information came to light long after he had died. The extraordinary story of Francisco de Cuellar, who lived in the sixteenth century, is documented in many sources in Ireland but most comprehensively through the letter he wrote, which is now a treasured item in a Spanish museum.

## MARGARET HAUGHERY

Who can know the span of their life or the ebb and flow of its journey? In the nineteenth century, tens of thousands of people abandoned their sparse livelihoods in Ireland in the desperate hope that something better might be possible in the new 'promised land' of America. For many, it was just another kind of drudgery in a strange land with a different climate. The new country brought the challenges of a relentless search for work, somewhere to live, land to cultivate, and food for large families. It would have been nothing less than a struggle, and the vast sweep of Atlantic Ocean separating them from the land of their birth made it all but impossible to pack up and return to family and familiarity when homesickness took a hold.

Amongst those making the decision to depart from all things familiar, with that heart's wish for better prospects, were five members of a family called Gaffney from Tully, near Carrigallen in the south of County Leitrim.

The story begins in the year 1813. On Christmas Day, a fifth child was born to William and Margaret Gaffney of Tully South. William was a small farmer and possibly a tailor. His wife Margaret (née O'Rourke) was a direct descendant of the O'Rourkes of Breiffne, the family who ruled the kingdom from which Leitrim was formed.

After a series of disastrously wet summers and failed crops, life became so challenging that the Gaffneys were amongst many who decided that emigration might be their only salvation. Taking three of their children – Margaret, then aged five, an older brother Kevin and the newest arrival, Kathleen – the couple set out on a storm-filled, six-month voyage to the land in which they invested their hopes and dreams for a more promising future. The remaining children stayed with an uncle, Matthew O'Rourke, until they could be sent for.

William found work as a carter at the docks in Baltimore and sent home money for the upkeep of the children left behind, as well as savings towards their passage to America. Sadly, within a short time of their arrival in Baltimore, the baby, Kathleen, died. Then disaster struck a deeper blow when an epidemic of yellow fever ravaged Baltimore in 1822. Both William and his wife Margaret were among the thousands who died and all of their possessions were burned to try to stop the spread of the disease. (Strangely, twenty-seven years later, a prayer book that somehow survived was returned to the family.)

Young Margaret was now nine. Her brother Kevin disappeared in the traumatic days following their parents' death. A fellow passenger from the voyage to America heard of the young girl's need for a home and took her in. Margaret worked for her keep and had very little education. She soon went into domestic service and the next date of consequence is 1835, when she married Charles Haughery. He was a man of poor health and the couple decided to see if the warmer climes of New Orleans would suit him better. They left within weeks of getting married and set up home there. Sadly, the therapeutic gains of the change of climate were short-lived. It was suggested that a sea voyage might help his condition and so Charles decided to go to Ireland, which may have been his homeland. He delayed the journey until after the birth of their first child, a daughter, then he left America, never to see his wife and daughter again as he died shortly after arriving in Ireland. Worse was to follow – the baby Frances died a few months later.

In Margaret's own words: 'My God! Thou hast broken every tie. Thou has stripped me of all. Again I am all alone.'

She was still only a young woman of twenty-three years old, with no parents, husband or child. Her brother was gone forever and she had no knowledge of her remaining siblings who had been left behind in Ireland. She had to find a new purpose for living and this is where the critical turning point came to change the life of a struggling, prematurely widowed Irish immigrant into a much-loved heroine who would be lauded by the poor, the rich, the Pope and state governors – and now, in the twentieth century, people who live in the community of her birth.

Perhaps as a result of her own deeply traumatic experience of being orphaned in a strange land, Margaret's attention was drawn to the acute needs of the many hundreds of orphans in New Orleans. She left the job she had to help out at the Poydras Orphan Asylum, run by the Sisters of Charity. Her first task was to collect food donations. She then became involved in helping the orphanage to relocate to a new building, and her astute ideas about fundraising and organisation resulted in her becoming the manager of the orphanage. However, within a short time the landlord sold the building and the orphan family had to find a new home. Margaret found one, beyond the city limits, in a house on a deserted plantation. This too carried her hallmark of successful enterprise, beginning with her ideas to buy a few cows so they could provide fresh milk for the orphans. Within a short time she had built up the stock into a dairy of forty cows, with butter, cream and milk being sold to raise much-needed income for the orphanage. And of course, the young orphans gained experience in dairy work, which added to the formal and practical education and handiwork classes that Margaret organised for them, to give them the best chance of finding work when they grew up and left the security of the orphanage.

The dairy was just the beginning of her enterprising zeal, because in 1840 Margaret was able to organise enough public support for a purpose-built orphanage.

Another yellow fever outbreak in the mid-1850s created an enormous quantity of orphaned babies and children. Margaret's answer to this was to secure public subscription for a home for babies, which opened in 1862.

In a strange turn of events, Margaret serendipitously became the owner of a bakery when the owner, to whom she had lent funds, went bankrupt. As the principal shareholder, it fell to her to try to save the business to try to recover her lost funds. Margaret's Bakery, as it became known, was an overnight success and it is from this that she made the greater part of her fortune, providing bread for all the assylums in New Orleans at rock-bottom prices. Her entrepreneurial gifts meant that she was always looking for improvements to the way the bakery was run. It became a state-of-the-art, first-of-its-kind steam bakery, regarded by all as a marvel. She gave bread to the poorest and most destitute who came to her door, ingeniously always cutting the bread in half so it couldn't be sold in exchange for alcohol.

The Civil War in the 1860s brought much devastation, not least more waves of orphans. Nonetheless, Margaret was able to negotiate safe passage for her flour deliveries so that she could keep her business running. Everything flourished, including her charitable work, keep-

ing little for herself and known to live quite simply. She was relentless in her desire to support the work of the orphanages and was instrumental in the building of other homes in the 1850s and 1860s.

In 1881, in her late sixties, Margaret contracted an unknown and incurable disease. She was cared for by her friends in the Sisters of Charity for many months and was visited by the poor and the rich, and clergy and politicians – Pope Pius IX sent his blessing and a crucifix. Margaret died on 9 February 1882. The New Orleans newspapers were edged in black. Her body was laid out in state and her funeral was attended by the highest in State office and the lowliest in social standing. Her funeral cortege brought the Stock Exchange to a standstill and the streets were thronged with orphans and dignitaries. The church where Requiem Mass was held was so crowded it was hard to get her coffin along the aisle.

Archbishop Perché, in his eulogy to Margaret, said: 'I have already been asked whether Margaret Haughery, who lived and labored so long and well amongst us, was a saint. It is not for me to make a pronouncement. But, if you put this same question to yourselves, dear brethren, you may find an answer similar to that which a little boy once made when a sister in our Sunday school enquired that somebody define a saint. "I think," said the child, remembering the human figures in stained glass windows, "that a saint is one who lets the light shine through".'

Margaret left all her wealth to charities, with the exception of the bakery, which was bequeathed to her foster son.

The City of New Orleans did not want to forget their precious Margaret, so a committee was set up to oversee the erection of a statue to her memory. Their high standards resulted in the first statue being returned to Italy, due to the inferior quality of the marble, and a replacement demanded. The second one was duly created and officially unveiled in July 1884, fittingly by children from every orphanage in the city. It was paid for in nickels and dimes – no large donations were accepted. The statue says, simply,

MARGARET. It was the first monument to be erected in America in honour of a woman.

Margaret's story was not forgotten in the Carrigallen area. Joe Doonan, a former principal of Carrigallen National School, kept the story on the school curriculum and thus it was known within the community for many years. More recently, a committee was formed to oversee the renovation of a property, believed to be Margaret's birthplace at Tully. Her life story was transformed into a highly successful play by Leitrim Youth Theatre Company under the direction and creativity of talented local playwright Maura Williamson and with songs by local singer and songwriter Tony Fahy. Strong links with people in New Orleans have been fostered and Margaret is more alive today in Carrigallen folk memory than ever before.

With the bicentenary of her birth celebrated in 2013, it seems that her story will run on as long as there is breath in Carrigallen.

Who could have known that this young emigree, taking her place amongst the thousands of desperate people arriving in America nearly 200 years ago in search of a new beginning, was destined to make such a positive contribution to the life of thousands of people, especially orphaned children – the many-named Margaret of Carrigallen, Angel of the Delta, Bread Lady of New Orleans … St Margaret?

## JACK BIRCHALL

It is said that 'truth is often stranger than fiction'. What follows is a glimpse into the fascinating account of a poor labourer, Jack Birchall, who was wrongly convicted of murder and hanged at Roscommon in 1829. Two 'threads' of evidence provide peculiar proof of his innocence: one, a manuscript held in Trinity College Library and the other, literally, a length of the rope that hung him. For almost two centuries, that fatal rope has brought healing to thousands of people touched by it and this, in its own way, has convinced all who heard the story that Birchall was an innocent victim of perjury.

So who was Jack Birchall and why should this story stand out so strongly in folk memory? The surname is recognisable to this day in Drumshanbo. The Protestant owners of the Blackrock Estate on the outskirts of the town were originally Lindsays, until the last of the Lindsays married Toby Birchall, also a Protestant. The subsequent estate owners were known as Lindsay Birchall. It is believed that Jack was the son of Henry, who in turn was an illegitimate son of either Toby or Robert Birchall. Toby was known for his 'extra mural' activities.

Jack Birchall was about twenty when his life was cut short when he was found guilty of murdering Thomas Cox, the manager of the Arigna Ironworks, a crime he denied. On 23 February 1828 a group of men attempted to steal gold which Cox had received to pay his English workforce at the Arigna Ironworks. The men approached Cox's house in the middle of the night and called out to him. The moment Cox raised his bedroom window and put out his head, he was fatally shot. Cox's quick-thinking sister put the gold into a crock of cream, resulting in a fruitless search by the robbers when they subsequently ransacked the house.

Two men employed at the ironworks – Tom Glynn, the night-watchman, and Jim Beirne, a teacher and private tutor – swore that Birchall was very much involved in the shooting of Cox. Both men were implicated in the robbery/murder but needed to construct an alibi to save their own lives. It was their questionable evidence that finally convicted young Birchall.

At the time of his conviction, Birchall lived in a small house with three brothers and a sister. His siblings claimed that their brother was at home asleep at the time of the murder, but this was overshadowed by the compelling, sworn evidences of Glynn and Beirne. However, it took three trials before Birchall was convicted. At the third trial the judge was one of the best judges of his day:

the Hon. Baron Smith. Handing down the sentence of death, on Friday, 7 August 1829, Smith was said to have pronounced the sentence 'in the most pathetic strain'.

On the day of his execution, 10 August 1829, outside the new Roscommon Courthouse, twenty-year-old Jack Birchall professed his innocence to the crowds and said from the scaffold: 'As I am an innocent man, bring home the rope that will hang me for it will have a cure in it.'

A friend of Birchall's, John Morrison, heard Jack's plea and, after the hangman's grim work was finished, asked for a length of the rope. The story goes that, on his way home, he stopped for a rest in the house of a woman who had a terrible ulcer on her leg. He remembered the piece of rope in his pocket and offered it to the woman, as nothing prescribed previously had managed to make her well. She accepted his offer. A few days later, Morrison was in the neighbourhood and called in to find out how she was faring. Remarkably, there was an improvement and he applied the rope to her ulcer several more times in the coming days and weeks and she fully recovered.

It is here that the rope takes on a life of its own. It has been passed on through the Morrison family, who lived in the Gowel area, east of Leitrim village, for two centuries. Hundreds, if not even thousands, of people have made use of its curing properties, and the thinnest remnant of that well-used hangman's rope still remains to this day. Those who believe in the power of cures have no difficulty in seeing this as sufficient evidence of Jack Birchall's innocence.

However, a local historian, Des Guckian, from Dromod, County Leitrim, felt compelled to delve more deeply into Jack Birchall's case, and, after piecing together all the available evidence in newspapers and court proceedings, he published his definitive account in 2012 under the title *Not Even a Sparrow Shall Fall: The Cruel Fate of Jack Birchall.*

While Des Guckian was researching the story, a local history lecture in Carrick-on-Shannon in 2007 came to his notice. It was delivered by Professor Roger Stalley of Trinity College Dublin and was on the work of Daniel Charles Grose, an English topographical artist, engraver and author who travelled all over Ireland and who had lived nearby in Annaduff for a number of years and died in Carrick-on-Shannon in 1838. In 1991, Professor Stalley had published Daniel Grose's *The Antiquities of Ireland: A Supplement to Francis Grose*, a hitherto unpublished work. In his talk, Professor Stalley referred to illustrations which Daniel Grose had done around the Arigna area and to Grose's 'Writing an account of the murder of the manager of Ironworks and the wrongful hanging of a young man for it'. Des Guckian found the manuscript at Trinity College Dublin. It was the final piece of evidence he needed to prove Birchall's innocence. The manuscript told that, on his deathbed a few years after the trial, Tom Glynn confessed that it was he who had shot dead Mr Cox and then framed Jack Birchall.

Des Guckian sees a much bigger political drama being played out through this case than the mere activities of some local would-be-robbers in Drumshanbo. He refers to the national political back-drop of 1798 when local yeomen and rebels, supported by the French, clashed strongly in that area. Referring to the obvious sectarian divide in the period 1828-29, Guckian states in his book: 'The subsequent capital punishment of Jack Birchall and the far more lenient sentences given to the other accused may well be explained by reference to the nasty bigoted way in which the smaller but state-backed Church of Ireland and the larger and emergent Roman Catholic Church locked horns in deadly combat just at that very time of the Catholic Emancipation struggle around the years 1828-29. The Protestants had recently begun a new evangelical movement called "The Second Reformation" and one supposes that to support the cause of an "illegitimate" might not have been "politically correct".'

The *Roscommon and Leitrim Gazette* and other unionist papers decried the murder and demanded a conviction. The more obviously guilty men had the backing of influential priests, such as Daniel O'Connell's friend and supporter Fr Tom Maguire from nearby Drumkeerin. The Catholic accused, through the influence of the priests, ended up with lesser sentences.

I'll end this tale of the unfortunate Jack Birchall with some words from a ballad, 'Burchall's Lamentation', which is still known in the Mount Allen area, west of Drumshanbo and close to where he lived:

> Burchall's Lamentation sounds through all the nation,
> His father's desolation I mean to let you know;
> Drumshanbo, Keash and Leitrim, it grieves me for to leave,
> When I think of those false traitors who have sent me to my grave.
> Tom Glynn did all he could, he was fond of human blood;
> Three Assizes there he stood, till at last he ended me,
> Now I am going to die upon the gallows tree,
> I'm as innocent of Cox's murder as the child upon your knee.

# FRANCISCO DE CUELLAR: A REMARKABLE SURVIVOR

When the great Spanish Armada set out to try to overthrow Elizabeth l of England in 1588, the plan was foiled by a combination of thwarted attacks, re-routing the return voyage to Spain of the 130 ships, storms in the North Sea and shipwrecks. More than twenty-four vessels were wrecked on the coasts of Ireland and altogether about fifty ships did not make it back to Spain.

When the storms off the north-west coast of Ireland struck the ships, some of the ships anchored close to the coast to try to sit out the worst. But the severe weather battered them and pushed many of them on to the rocks. Most of the occupants of the stricken ships were lost at sea and, for those who survived drowning, worse was yet to come. The local Irish, as well as the hundreds of locally-garrisoned English soldiers, wasted little time in massacring any survivors they laid their hands on. Bodies were stripped of wealth – many had gold coins sewn into their clothes and valuable jewellery round their necks.

In the most extraordinary of circumstances, verging on the completely miraculous, one particular sea captain survived the storm, survived several beatings and attacks from both native Irish and English troops, and even survived a second storm when he finally secured passage for the journey home on a ship that was headed for Antwerp. The reason all this is known now, with incredible accuracy, is that not only did the amazing survivor write down his awful adventure, but aspects of it were also passed down through both the oral and written sources of North West Ireland.

His name was Francisco de Cuellar and his name is very well-known in the areas around north Leitrim and Sligo where he found some refuge, even while his life continued to remain at great risk. De Cuellar was born in the mid-to-late 1500s. He was in the army that conquered Portugal in 1581, he sailed in the frigate, the *Santa Catalina*, to the Strait of Magellan and was in Brazil expelling French settlers.

Extraordinarily, he had been sentenced to death just before the storm struck for the crime of breaking out of formation. For whatever reason, the sentence was not carried out and, when the disastrous storms rose up, it was every man for himself. The ship he was on was driven on to Streedagh Strand off the north-west coast of the present County Sligo.

De Cuellar managed to escape the sinking ship and was advised by the scarce few helpful people he met to head for the castle of Brian O'Rourke of Breffni in the mountains of what is now north Leitrim, where some survivors were already in safe refuge. He stayed some time there, leaving once with a group of fellow sailors to try to get on board a ship that was still intact, but they failed to make the connection and many of the people he travelled with on that perilous journey to the ship were also murdered on the way.

He returned to O'Rourke's stronghold and remained there some time before moving on to the territory of the MacClancys, probably at Rosclogher near Lough Melvin. When news came of a huge army of English heading for MacClancy's castle, the Spaniards, including de Cuellar, offered to defend it whilst the Irish went into hiding. The courageous Spanish had nothing to lose but their lives and they had survived this far by the wiles of destiny.

The English besieged the castle for many days, until a snowstorm forced them to retreat. When the MacClancys returned, they were grateful beyond words and de Cuellar was offered MacClancy's daughter in marriage as a thank you. He declined and shortly afterwards, in the thick of winter, he and a group of Spaniards went on their way again. Some say they sneaked away from the castle, so as not to offend their host.

The next place of refuge was with the Bishop of Derry and a safe passage to Scotland was found for de Cuellar and other Spaniards who had arrived earlier in the north of Ireland. In Scotland, another long wait was necessary – this time of several months while he waited for the Duke of Parma to get him a safe passage to Flanders.

Within sight of the harbour a Dutch fire attack caused de Cuellar's ship to be lost and once again he survived by clinging on to wreckage, finally managing to complete his journey home. But de Cuellar's war services were far from over and to the end of his life he continued to be involved in siege after siege.

How and when he died is not known, nor if he had any children. It is likely that he died in the early 1600s.

Of his supporters in Ireland, O'Rourke was hanged in London in 1590 for treason, among his alleged crimes being his support of the Spanish survivors. MacClancy was captured in 1590 and beheaded.

### Postscript

The letter that Francisco de Cuellar wrote of his adventures on his return to mainland Europe remained unpublished until the late nineteenth century, and since then it has been regarded as a valuable document of its time by historians and academics. The original letter is kept in the Royal Academy of History in Madrid as part of the collection of Luis Salazar. An English translation of de Cuellar's letter can be seen at www.ucc.ie/celt/published/T108200/index.html.

In 2010, Spanish writer José Luis Gil Soto published a historical novel called *The Hill of White Stones*, which is based on the events of the Spanish Armada's voyage.

## The Poet Higgins

In connection with my work as a storyteller, I had often heard mention locally in Leitrim of 'The Poet Higgins' (in that form, not as Patrick Higgins, his actual name). It was clear from snippets that I saw that his commentaries – both of happenings long before his time and of contemporary events – formed a considerable treasury of life in rural Ireland up to the late nineteenth century. However, apart from a few poems dotted here and there in local jottings, school reunion books and the Irish Folklore Commission's schools archive of 1937-38, no single collection of his work had taken place. By good fortune for this publication, the fullest collection of his poems was published in 2011 by the newly-formed Poet Higgins Society, which came into being with the specific intention of creating the definitive collection. The poet's descendants in America were contacted and brought back in touch with their Irish connections. A permanent landmark, marking his life from 1832-1902, is now in place on the 'Poet's Hill' at Cloncoose in County Leitrim, where Higgins had spent his whole life, close to the historic village of Ballinamuck in neighbouring County Longford.

Many of his poems had been written down by John Bohan, a close friend of the poet. They were kept safe and they contributed greatly to the 2011 publication, which was edited by Kathleen Duffy, a granddaughter of Bohan, who is also the copyright holder. In her introduction, Kathleen describes him thus:

> … the poet was a man rooted in the soil of Cloncoose. He did not allow his poetic genius to come between himself and his neighbours. Through his poems he puts the artisans on a par with the poet, by lauding their skills. His poems on local people: Patrick Doignan, the shopkeeper; Jack Keenan, the craftsman; Sheeran, the young tailor…all show his sense of pride in his local community. He uses hyperbole and epic boasting to laud and celebrate the skilled craftsmanship …

In tribute to his work, I have selected, with permission from Kathleen Duffy, three poems which form a sketch of the times in and around the Leitrim-Longford border lands which were Higgins' canvas.

### 'Tom Gilheaney'

'Tom Gilheaney' is Higgins' best known poem. The adventures of young Gilheaney are set against the background of the 1798 freedom campaign. This young pikeman is betrayed by his fellow countryman, Shuffling Shawn, into the hands of a Yeoman. But the stranger's honour leads him to spare Gilheaney. This tale sings itself along on its journey and is a great history lesson, as well as one in the importance of a strong moral character, and as you'll see, one good deed deserves another.

It happened once upon a time,
As sages tell in phrase sublime,
That Tom Gilheaney stout and straight
Prepared his pike in ninety-eight,
And from Drumkeeran did advance
To join the gallant sons of France.
Thus hastily equipped for war
He journeyed on to Castlebar,
Where there he showed good Irish play
Before the Saxons ran away.
It made him joyful to behold
The flutter of the green and gold,
And oftentimes that day he said,
Thank God the green waves o'er the red.

Next morning for Collooney then
He marched with the Killala men,
Where victory again did smile
Upon the banners of our Isle.
The rank and file, with lances long,
Unfailing nerves and sinews strong,
The vengeful mandate did obey
Which made them victors of the day.

To see how foemen reeled and ran
Was balsam for an Irishman.
Besides the band conjointly played,
In thundering strains, 'The White Cockade'.
And brilliant was Gilheaney's luck,
Till he arrived at Ballinamuck.

'Til by reverse of fortune there
He had to fly in wild despair
O'er hill and valley, mead and moor,
His life not for a moment sure.
That night beneath a hedge he lay,
Until it was approaching day.

When stepping forward at the dawn,
He met a man called Shuffling Shawn
To whom he did communicate
His sore distress and helpless state,
And that he did not break his fast
For eight and forty hours past.

Shawn brought him to his cosy cot
And for him good refreshments got.
He pleased the refugee so well
He did his whole adventures tell:
'I have some money here to spare
That you might take unto your care
Though all my lot may ill become,
Pray let my parents have the sum.'

The money, being such tempting stuff,
Was freely taken sure enough.
And when he started you must know
Shawn pointed out the road to go
And told him where he might be sure
To rest some days and lay secure.

Gilheaney seemed well satisfied
And bid good morning to his guide.
But when he reached the distant place
A yeoman stared him in the face
And uttered out in tones severe:
'Damn Papish dog! What brought you here?'

'A rebel you were in the past
But now your doom is sealed at last
Bob Ferguson it is my name
And I don't think it sin or shame
A Croppy dog like you to swing
Who proved a traitor to his king.'


Gilheaney then spoke up and said:
'I see too late I am betrayed.
Although your worst I do not fear,
Curse on the man that sent me here.
He got my money and it is plain
He thus contrived to get me slain.'


Those words then seemed to mollify
The yeoman's rage, he did reply:
'I shall investigate this case
So now your steps you must retrace.'
He took with him a loaded gun,
Lest that Gilheaney off might run.


So onward then through brake and bawn
They went until they came to Shawn
Whom Ferguson did then accost
Without one moment's time being lost:
'Have you got money, let me know,
From this man here, not long ago?'


'At least to me he so pretends
So it's on your word his life depends.'
Shawn uttered in a sulky tone:
'I have no money but my own.
And have his money, tell me how
Can I who saw him not till now?'
Gilheaney did him then confront
With gestures and expressions blunt:

'You know,' said he, 'you undertook
To care my cash and pocket book
And besides it's written on the seam
The full initials of my name.'

The yeoman said: 'Then I will try
To see who's guilty of the lie
And he that is will shortly see
The regions of eternity.'
Shawn trembled then from limb to limb
And stammered out: 'I believe it's him.'

'He gave to me, I must confess,
Four pounds and nothing more or less
And if you wish the same to count
Just here it is, the full amount.'

'This bloody traitor, worst of men,'
Retorted the fierce yeoman then,
'To keep the paltry sum, you would,
Were I but rash and spill his blood.

'But now I am proud to say,
Gilheaney will not die today
He can go on and choose his road
Or come this night to my abode.
And if he does I'll let him see
That shelter he will get from me.'

So what occurred between the pair
I shall just by and by declare.
When thirty days and nights passed round
Gilheaney was both safe and sound
And Ferguson, when the fight was o'er,
Took up his spade and scythe once more.

But henceforth let what will betide,
The faults of Bob or Shawn don't hide.
The fearless youngster took his leave
And many hearty blessings gave.
Besides he said when going away:
'Perhaps we'll meet some other day.'

Then for his native home with speed,
In spirits high he did proceed,
And in his course no hobble met
Till he arrived before sunset.
His parents met him at the door
With stretched out hands, you may be sure.

He told them all that he went through
The very same as I told you
And how the whole affair did pass
'Twixt Bob and Shawn at Aughavas.

The old man's passion grew so hot
He sized his baitín on the spot
And made a flourish round about
And like a deer he started out.

His consort asked where he was going
But he replied, 'Let me alone.
A wink I'll neither stand nor stop,
Nor break my fast nor taste a drop,
Nor sleep, till I give Shawn a lick
Or two of this good thorny stick.'

Then Tom looked up with childish glee
And says at this: 'Leave Shawn to me.'
The good old fellow there and then
Desisted and returned in
And did no further freaks display
When the excitement died away.

Soon rolled around thrice seven years
With all their joys, with all their tears,
When Ferguson did then prepare
And started for Drumkeeran Fair.
And like a burly business man
To buy a horse he there began.

But when the bargain it was made
Another man stepped in and said:
'I'll keep this horse and you may try
Another of his kind to buy.'
Sure Ferguson did long contend
Without assistance of a friend.

'Till he got overawed and cowed
At the appearance of the crowd.
At length a man asked for his name
And for the place from whence he came
His answer was: 'I'm far from home
And to you all I am unknown
But then no rebel I might fear
If Tom Gilheaney had been here.'
A lusty voice did then cry out:
'Pray tell what this is all about
For if not mentioned for a ban
The word Gilheaney, here I am.'

'Now Tom avic,' the yeoman said,
I think I'm worthy of your aid
At least I'm sure you must allow
If that you do but know me now.'
So when he took a look at Bob
He says to him: 'Fear not this mob.

'Because your case I'll rectify
At any cost were I to die.
The horse he grappled by the head
And the intruders quickly fled.

Gilheaney brought him home that night
To all his neighbours' great delight.

They spent that night in mirth and cheer
Until the daylight did appear,
When Ferguson he did repeat:
'I'm proud I lived in ninety-eight.
I'm glad Gilheaney did not die
So now I bid you all goodbye.'

## 'Peter Bawn'

The effects of eviction run rife in Irish history. Here though, Higgins tells a tale with a lovely twist that brings a much happier, if rarer, solution that thousands of evicted tenants might only have dreamed about.

Aroused from sleep at early dawn
On Christmas Eve was Peter Bawn.
A knock came to his window sill
Close followed by the words: 'I'm chill.
I have been all the night astray
From early dusk till break of day,
And though to no one here akin
I hope to be admitted in.'

Old Peter answered, 'Woe is me,
This day completes my misery,
Though weak and worn down with age
On me the tyrant vents his rage.
This night's repose I am denied
Here where my father lived and died.
A case more sad was never known,
For I am helpless and alone.

Alas, my children, all but one,
Are many years both dead and gone;

And he that still does life retain
Will never here return again
Because he thinks my hoary head
Is long since numbered with the dead.'
The twang of the evicting force
Here terminated this discourse.

And then the owner of the land
Appeared himself in chief command
Well mounted on a prancing steed
Right for the door he did proceed.
And with a supercilious air
He asked was he occupier there
Or had he cash prepared to pay
His legal dues without delay.

The stranger then in accent clear
Proclaimed aloud: 'The cash is here,
And the whole sum, what'er it be
Forthwith shall be advanced by me.'
The lordling then with sullen brow
Inquired thus: 'Whence comest thou?'
The answer was: 'It brings no shame
On me to tell from whence I came.

I am a traveller from afar
That bore the test of toil and war,
I braved the shocks of field and foam
And now I'm at my native home.
Besides, I am, I do confess,
The old man's son whom you oppress,
But I shall make his home this night
Resound with joy and glow with light.

And he shall henceforth live in peace
In his ancestral dwelling place
Which is endeared to him, I ween,
By many a sad and joyous scene.'
The landlord here got his demand
And father, son went hand in hand
Into the old abode and then
They wept for joy like ransomed men.

## 'Lines on a Tailor'

A poem which celebrates the skilled craftsmanship of a young tailor boy, Sheeran.

You foppish lads of high renown
That's in the dandy line,
I pray excuse my feeble muse
And with me now combine
To celebrate a tailor boy,
Once more I do begin.
To celebrate his needlework
I had to mend my pen
Though this worthy lad a juvenile
Extensive is his fame
He lately left this country
And Sheeran is his name.
The tailors of this country
Bewail his great uprise
Saying now we'll lose our customers
Who wear fine clothes and frieze,
For we were held in great esteem
And that not long ago
But it's now we'd hardly get
A drugget breeches for to sew
For he cuts his cloth with judgement

All in geometric line
And by his scale and measure
He does chalk and mark his signs
He made his work in fashion
Both comely, neat and gay
No wrinkle, crease or pucker
Could any man displease.
He makes jackets and long trousers
And handsome pantaloons
For soldiers and for officers,
For sailors and dragoons.
He makes fashionable leggings
Surmounting handsome boots,
Waistcoats and body coats,
And elegant surtouts.
He makes galloses and breeches,
Big coats and bang-ups too
And what he goes to mend
He makes it equal as if new.
All masculine attirement
He fits in proper style,
All sorts he fits in sizes
From a giant to a child.
It's then he fits the ladies
In mantles and in jocks
In riding coats, pelisses
In morning gowns and frocks.
And what he makes of every kind
It's tedious for to tell
He makes them so exquisite
There is none can him excel.
And as for his needlework
He does it neat and sure.
Often time botched workmanship

He's called upon to cure
For he fits them to a nicety
Tho' never apt to squeeze,
All joints he leaves at liberty,
Fork elbows and the knees.
There are captains of militia bands
And lords of high renown
Have written for Mr Sheeran
To go to Dublin town.
Young lads whom we call bachelors
Who are looking for a wife
Are inquiring for Sheeran
As a help to change their lives
For he makes them look so decent-like
So splendid and so trig
He makes them look majestical
Suppose they are not big.
So if we send for Sheeran
Before we have the wars
I think he won't refuse me
For to make a pair of drawers.


## REFERENCES

**Margaret Haughery:** Retold with permission using content from the website created for the Carrigallen-based Margaret of New Orleans committee. The material, originally written and researched by Raymond Hackett and Michael Reilly, was first published in *Carrigallen Parish – A History* (1996). www.margaretsbirthplace.com.
**Jack Birchall:** Story retold with permission from Des Guckian, author of *Not Even a Sparrow Shall Fall – The Cruel Fate of Jack Birchall*. A copy of his well-researched book may be purchased by writing to him at Des Guckian, Dromod, County Leitrim.

**Francisco de Cuellar:** various internet sources, including Wikipedia.

**The Poet Higgins:** Used with permission from Kathleen Duffy, editor and copyright holder, *Patrick Higgins (1832-1902): Poet of the Leitrim-Longford Borderlands*. Published by The Poet Higgins Society, Cloncoose, Co Leitrim 2011. ISBN 978-0-9569908-0-8. Tom Gilheaney, p5, Peter Bawn, p3, Lines on a Tailor, p32. www. poethiggins.com.

# 6

# Strange Floods, Tragic Drownings, Overflowing Wells – and a Merman

## The Second Great Flood

On a drive around rural Leitrim, the general vista is mainly empty fields and bare hills, with small farms dotted across the landscape. It is hard to imagine the county well-populated, which it was up until the mid-1800s when the 1841 census returned 155,000 people. There are many reasons for the drastic fall in the county's residents to the present figure of just under 32,000.

A major recession caused by the mechanisation of linen weaving in the 1830s changed working patterns and livelihoods for many people. Sharply followed by this was the Great Famine between 1845 and 1852. Death and mass emigration followed and the busy activity of the hard-won life on fields and hillsides subsided and quieted.

However, there is a quirky story about a once-thriving town on the Leitrim-Cavan borderland that suddenly disappeared – and its vanishing in every form had nothing to do with industrialisation or hunger. Rather, its demise is said to be due to an act of God.

An economically-successful village, Tober had a school, a chapel, a mill and a market house, as well as many tradespeople such as millers, hatters, weavers, nailers, carpenters and coopers.

Every year on 15 August a pattern or pilgrimage was held there and the village was positively buzzing with the many visitors who made the special trip for that celebration. But underneath this vibrant and holy event there were always rumblings and petty jealousies between rival families that came to the surface on these busy festival days.

It is said that on one of these pattern days, an apple dealer tossed some apples into the river. Some small boys jumped in to get the fruit and began to fight. Soon the river was full of people who jumped in to support their relatives and one thing led to another, resulting in a massive, rowdy and dangerous water battle. The fight was so fierce that the river ran red with blood.

A few years later, on another busy pattern day, much the same happened again, and this time the fight resulted in a man having his leg broken. The local parish priest was furious that the religious ceremony was being used as an excuse to vent tribal disagreements and it is said that he cursed the people who performed stations at the well.

From then on, the big annual gatherings stopped and fewer and fewer people made the journey to Tober. As a result, there was a massive decline in the economy of the village and the family rivalries became more and more bitter.

The final and peculiar destruction of the once-thriving village came on 22 June 1861. A terrific storm with thunder, lightning and torrential rain – considered by local people as a curse from God – brought in its wake the very worst of floods, yet only on the small area around Tober.

The huge run of water in spate ran into the houses, rising as high as the rafters. People pulled out windows to let out the water and try to save their homes. It is said that when one of the rival families suffered the complete loss of their home and possessions, they noticed that the home of a family from the other clan was still surviving.

So they made sure the losses would be felt by their 'enemies' too and breached the wall of that house, causing the water to surge through. No sympathies were spared, even in a time of great need.

When the strange, localised storm stopped and people were able to see the damage, it was clear that most of the village was ruined and possessions and livelihoods lost. For weeks afterwards, bales of linen, barrels and baskets were seen floating down the Shannon, whose early reaches are close to Tober and its connecting streams.

During the flood, the water in the well rose at least a metre above its normal level, circling up the trunk of an old ash tree beside it. The weight of the water against the tree caused it to topple over and half cover the well. When the well water finally returned to normal the tree was cut down, but the wood was never burned as it was regarded as sacred.

Today it is as hard to picture the throbbing activity of Tober as it is to imagine Leitrim's countryside in its heyday of being highly populated and industrious, but such is the cycle of life. The stories are all that remain.

However, when one thing ends, another thing begins and many of Tober's homeless families rebuilt their lives in what is now the present village of Dowra. It is the first village on the River Shannon, marking the uppermost navigable point on the river. The river marks the line of the Cavan-Leitrim county boundary. The approach to the village from the south, on the east side of Lough Allen, is in County Leitrim all the way to the bridge across the river. Then, upon crossing it into Dowra, Cavan begins.

Dowra's name in Irish, An Damhshraith, means 'the shrine of the ox' and an old tradition suggests that droves of oxen or bullocks grazed along the river. A line of stepping stones over the river created a good crossing point and one of the first businesses to emerge at the new settlement was a blacksmith's, to shoe horses for those en route to the ford. Other businesses, including a nailer, a miller and basket-makers, established and soon all the usual trades, dealers and shopkeepers of the day found their way to Dowra and the village grew.

# AN EASTER TRAGEDY

The lives of many families living at the northern end of Lough Allen were turned upside down one Easter weekend when a regular shopping trip resulted in a mass funeral.

Until tarred roads and cars became commonplace, one of the most common ways of travel was by water. For the people living on Lough Allen it was usual for them to make use of a weekly boat service from the northern end of the lake to the market town of Drumshanbo, some 18km away. People took with them the produce of their farms and kitchens, and with the money they earned they bought the provisions needed for home.

But on that fateful Good Friday in April 1831, the boat was caught in a storm on the return journey and all on board perished.

When the boat was ready to leave from the Corry shore on the morning of 2 April, twenty-five people were hoping to make the journey but there was only room for eighteen, so several people had to go by road or abandon their plans. They were the lucky ones.

The return journey from Drumshanbo should have begun at 3 p.m. but, for many reasons, the departure was delayed and did not get underway until 7 p.m.

When all the passengers who had made the outward trip embarked, the boat was very low in the water, due to the extra load of seed oats and potatoes required for the spring sowing. Accounts describe how a Mrs Forde, a regular passenger, felt uneasy and she and a neighbour, Paddy Travers, decided to leave the boat and remain in Drumshanbo overnight with friends. Two other passengers, from Ballinaglera, also decided not to make the homeward trip by boat and chose to walk home. These four were fated to live too.

The weather on leaving Drumshanbo was favourable but it quickly deteriorated and before long a strong gale was blowing, whipping up wind and waves. By now it was becoming dark and within a few kilometres of Drumshanbo the boat was seen from the shore to be in difficulty.

Overloaded and heavy in the water due to its unusually heavy cargo, the boat capsized quickly and all fourteen occupants were drowned. People who watched the tragedy from the shore scanned the water with lamps, hoping to spot survivors. At dawn the following morning, local men set out in boats and were able to recover all of the bodies – four men and ten women. They were brought back to Corry for bereaved relatives to claim and the coffins of all fourteen people were laid to rest together in a mass grave in Kilbride Cemetery. A large headstone was erected over the grave, naming all of the victims. One of them, Johnnie MacFadden, the captain of the boat, was to have been married on Easter Monday.

## 'SON OF THE BIRDS'

When the son of a Leitrim chieftain was refused the hand of the woman he loved, he lost hope and took to wandering.

He went from place to place until he came to the shores of a lough, where he built a simple shelter and resigned himself to the life of a hermit. He created and planted a garden for food and, to while away the lonely hours, he sat by the water and played his cláirsaich and sang.

The time passed. He continued with his simple existence. Little changed except that people who lived nearby heard his music and it touched their hearts. His singing was appreciated and soon he became known as 'mac ui n-éan', which means 'son of the birds'.

It so happened that his lost love, who remained unmarried, was accompanying her father through Glenfarne. The chieftain and his troops were intending to meet an enemy chieftain in battle. After a day's travelling they camped at Moneyduff, close to the shores of the lough where the prince-turned-hermit was living.

When the camp was set up, the woman went towards the lough and she heard the most beautiful chanting, singing and music. She followed the sounds through the trees and arrived at the tiny her-

mitage. She went closer to see who was playing, sensing a familiarity with what she heard. Indeed, she had found her long-lost prince.

The meeting between the clans took place and the prince-turned-hermit was called on to make a ruling during the battle that ensued. His wisdom was honoured and such was the impact of it that the chieftain who had earlier forbidden his daughter to marry the prince saw the error of his ways and changed his mind, allowing the much-desired marriage to take place.

Although the 'son of the birds' is no longer living by that lake-shore in north Leitrim, there is a haunting beauty in the sounds and in the stillness of the place. And the legacy of the prince who became the husband he longed to be is kept alive here in the telling of this story about how Lough MacNean got its name.

## The Prophecy of the Uncovered Well

It is said that many, many years ago there was a different village called Sligigh, or Sligo, to the east of the existing county town of that name. It was in a valley, in the area close to the boundaries between the two present counties of Leitrim and Sligo.

The story goes that, on the outskirts of the village, there was a spring well covered by a large flagstone. Anyone who took water from the well had to remember to firmly replace the flag and cover the well completely. Failing to do that would risk the fulfilment of a prophecy: that the attars or spirits of the well would cause the well to overflow and the village would be lost.

A girl went to the well one day and she forgot to cover it. That night, as everyone slept, a great flood surged from the well and the village was submerged. When morning came, not even a roof of the old village could be seen above the waters of the new lake that had formed.

This, people say, is how Lough Gill came into being. And some claim that, when the lake levels are low, the roofs of the old houses can still be seen.

## THE GLEN OF JEALOUSY

Long ago, in what is now north Leitrim, a woman became very jealous of her husband and she decided to cook him a dinner with the flesh of a poisonous creature she had fished out of the nearby lake.

He ate the meal and suspected nothing, but he soon fell ill and as he lay dying, she felt quite remorseful for what she had done. Her husband realised what had happened and he said to her that he would be able to recover if she sat naked on a large stone on the hillside for several hours. In her eagerness to undo the fate she had schemed for him, she did exactly as he suggested. She died doing this, bringing the death-wish to herself. Miraculously, he recovered, married again and lived happily to the end of his days.

This is one story that explains why Glenade is so-called because it means the 'glen of jealousy'.

Another story of the origin of the name of Glenade is this: two chieftains were passing through the area and as they stood at a place near a stream, their attention was caught by the direction of its course. What they saw was that the stream ran down the mountain to a certain point where it split into two streams. One ran on down the hillside and the other seemed to go upwards and disappear. They couldn't work it out, but they concluded that the streams must have quarrelled and parted and, as such, the area should be known as the 'glen of jealousy'.

## The Well that Chose its Own Course

A peculiar story surrounds the ownership of a well near Dromahair. It is said that the well was on the boundary between land owned by two farmers and was the cause of many bitter quarrels, as each farmer claimed the well was on his land.

Nothing could be resolved amicably out of court, so a case was prepared to try to bring the conflict to a conclusion.

The story goes that, on the morning when the case was to be heard, the well dried up completely in its original location and reappeared on some land that was apparently owned by no one …

Case dismissed.

## The Man who Defied his Landlord

In the days when tough landlords called the shots and families lived in constant fear of unaffordably high rents and, worse still, eviction, few happy tales would have been told about life on some large estates. But one that brings a smile amidst such adversity is always welcome, and so it goes with this tale about a man who lived on the estate of a south Leitrim landlord.

The story goes that the landlord took a fancy to the man's daughters and wanted them to be servants at his stately home.

The farmer dared to refuse his landlord and before he knew it he and his family were evicted.

None of his neighbours could give him refuge for fear of the same happening to them if they supported their impoverished friend.

The homeless farmer is said to have taken his family to an island on a nearby lake and there he built a house, as well as a timber road from the island to the land. When the landlord heard about this, he ordered bailiffs to block the rivers flowing out of the lake so that the lake water level rose and flooded the road.

The poor farmer, ever resourceful, then made a makeshift boat from rough planks tied together and managed to get back and forth from the island. The landlord, furious at being outwitted by the farmer, tried to get him evicted from the island – only to discover that the lake wasn't in his ownership.

Eventually, the landlord accepted the cleverness of his former tenant and reinstated him on the land, in a new house and with a few acres to farm that saw him happily to the end of his days.


## THE STRANGE CREATURES OF CLOONCORRICK LAKE

A simple boat trip into a lake to cut bulrushes turned into a never-to-be-repeated experience for a Leitrim farmer. Having set out in his boat on Clooncorrick Lake near Carrigallen, the farmer was certain he could see someone in the water swimming towards him. As the swimmer came closer, the farmer saw a fish tail and was alarmed at what might happen. He had a slash hook with him for cutting the bulrushes and he prepared to defend himself as best he could. Without hesitating, he lashed out at the half-man-half-fish and the slash hook lodged in his potential assailant's shoulder.

The injured creature disappeared and the farmer's first thought was to row back to the shore and to the safety of the land as quickly as he could, but instead he found himself jumping into the lake. Something in the water pulled him down to the floor of the lake and there he saw several more half-man-half-fish creatures. One of them seized him by the hand and pulled him deeper into the cavern of the lake bottom. By now the farmer was too afraid to resist and he seemed to have little choice but to do as he was bidden.

After swimming far they reached a network of caves, going deeper and deeper into what the farmer thought must be the hills surrounding the lake. There he was shown the injured half-man-half-fish and he was ordered to pull out the slash hook and rub his own hand over the injury on the shoulder in order to heal the wound. He did as instructed and was led back through the warren of caves to the bed of the lake.

The next thing the farmer knew, he was back in his own boat. He was weak and shaking and it took him all his strength to row back to the shore.

Whenever he needed bulrushes for thatching in the future, that was one lake he made sure to avoid.

## References

**The Second Great Flood:** main story re Tober – NFCS206:7. Cor na Gaoithe school. Teacher: Bean Úi Fhloinn. Also – Wikipedia.

**An Easter Tragedy:** www.cherithgospel.org/lovelyleitrim.htm; *Around Allen* by Michael Coppins edited by Fr Gerry Comiskey (1989).

**Son of the Birds:** NFCS198:30. Broca School. Teachers: T Ó Chioráin/S Ó Gallchobhair.

**The Prophecy of the Uncovered Well:** NFCS189:76; Mrs Ellen Parkes, Conrea, Gurteen PO, Manorhamilton, farmer's wife. Diffreen School.

**The Glen of Jealousy:** NFCS189:38; Pat McNulty (83), farmer, Carraduff, Glenade (stream) & PJ Rooney (60), farmer, Leclassor, Sligo (poisoning). Gleann Éada School. Teacher: Bean Uí Mhaolaith.

**The Well that Chose its Own Course:** NFCS201:208; Mrs MacCarrick, Dromahair. Collector: Patricia McGoldrick, Drumlease School. Teacher: Tomás Diolín.

**The Man who Defied his Landlord:** NFCS214:181; Pat Reynolds, Culmore, Dromod. Eanach Dubh (B) school. Teacher: Thomas Morahan; also NFCS217:39; Edward Faughnan (72), Cloonfannon, Dromod. Collector: Eileen Heeran, 13, Cloonturk GNS.

**The Strange Creatures of Clooncorrick Lake:** NFCS228:26; John Sheridan (67), Clonghla, Carrigallen. Carraig Áluinn school. Teacher: Pádhraic Maguidhir.

# 7

# MYTHICAL COWS, ENCHANTED COWS

Ireland and cows are inseparable. Cows have been part of life on the island since long before written records began, but as soon as they did, the early law texts, wisdom texts, sagas and stories of the saints were full of references to cattle, testifying to their importance in early Irish society.

Folk tales tell of cows which give unending supplies of milk to people in need and that are as quick to leave when their generosity is abused. Other stories are about milk failing to churn, often due to fairy involvement or some curses being placed on the cows. The stories all have a universal theme and though they might be ascribed to happening in a particular area, they are pretty much identical in subject matter. This chapter contains a few tales gathered from around the county.

Before telling the actual stories, I include some excerpts from a fascinating article about cattle in early Irish society, and I am grateful to its author, Shae Clancy, for giving me permission to include this.

In ancient Ireland, cattle, especially milch or milking cows, were the unit of currency and the measure of a person's status. The largest unit of currency in the old Irish system was the cumal, which was equivalent in value to a female slave or to three, or three and a half, milch cows. Similarly, a sét was valued at half a milch cow.

The early law texts describe penalties for wrongdoing in terms of numbers of cattle. For example, the fine for injuring a person's shin was three séts, which had to include a milch cow and a calf. Social status was an important part of Irish life. A man with only one cow was regarded as being extremely poor. The lowest grade of freeman who was non-royal had seven cows and a bull, whilst the highest grade had to have thirty cows to qualify for the status.

Early Irish cattle were mostly black, although red and brown are also mentioned. There are also references to brindled cows – those having more than one colour.

The colour combination most frequently mentioned in the sagas and lives of the saints is that of the white cow with red ears. St Brigid, as an infant, vomited all unclean food and the problem was solved when her druid father provided milk from a white, red-eared cow. In another story, a pious man's calf was eaten by a wolf, but St Finian ordered the wolf to fetch a calf to replace the one it had eaten. The wolf reappeared with a white red-eared calf.

Cows are frequently referred to in myths such as the Táin Bó Cúalnge – the Cattle Raid of Cooley – when the Morrigan attacked Cú Chulainn in the guise of a white red-eared heifer, and in the Wooing of Étaín, when Midir included fifty white red-eared cows in his stake during a game of chess.

However, they are not exclusive to mythology. There is a unique herd of red-eared white cattle in an enclosed park at Chillingham Park in north Northumberland in England. It is speculated they are descendants of feral cattle that were accidentally imprisoned when the park was enclosed from the surrounding forest in the thirteenth century. There are records of other similar herds in England and Wales that are now extinct.

The cattle raid was a social institution in Ireland. Nobles were praised during their lifetimes, and afterwards, for the number of raids they had carried out. Many place names owe their origin to cattle raids. Druim Cliabh or Drumcliffe, in County Sligo, is supposedly named after the wickerwork boats made there by a certain Caurnán in preparation for a raid. Ath Cliath Medraige, or Clarinbridge, in County Galway, is so-called because of the hurdles of thorns and brambles which the seven Maines, sons of Ailill and Medb, placed in the ford to delay those pursuing them after they had been on a raid in Munster.

Even the Christian clergy saw nothing wrong with cattle raids and some saints demanded a share of the plunder resulting from every raid launched from the territory in which their monasteries lay. St Caillín of Fenagh, for example, demanded a 'fat cow out of every prey' and even went so far as to threaten lack of success in raiding on those who refused him his share. And St Colmán Mac Luachán was regarded as the patron saint of cattle raiders.

On the other hand, cattle raids on monasteries were definitely not approved by the clergy, even though in most cases the animals were the property of tenants of the church. One example of a raid of this kind occurred in 994, when 2,000 cows were taken in a raid by the Airgialla on Armagh.

Probably the best-known cattle raids were those initiated by a newly inaugurated king who proved his worth by a raid into the territory of one of the traditional rivals or foes of his people. A special term, *creach rígh*, meaning 'king's raid', was used to describe the event, indicating that it was a normal part of the inauguration procedure.

The earliest recorded raid took place in 628, but there is no reason to believe that raiding was not part of normal life prior to that. The Annals of the Four Masters records over 500 unambiguous references to cattle raids between 854 and 1603. The number of cattle, almost always cows, taken in raids varied from a few to 'many thousand'. The highest number cited in the annals is 6,000, which were taken on a raid in Connaught in 1062.

## THE FIRST COWS IN IRELAND

Where did the first cows in Ireland come from originally? Here is a story that offers an answer.

Long ago, out of the Western Sea, a sea-maiden came ashore on the land of Ireland. She was well received wherever she went and treated with honour and dignity. She learned the language of the different people and began to explain to them that a great spirit had sent her to Ireland to announce the arrival of three goddesses who would come in the form of cows to bring fertility and prosperity to the land.

The cows would be different colours – Bó Ruadh (the red cow), Bó Dubh (the black cow) and Bó Fionn (the white cow) – and each would go to a different part of Ireland.

When the sea-maiden had told the good news across the land, she began to grow weary of life out of the water and longed to be reunited with her own people. She asked to be brought back to the sea and there, on a May eve, she was carried into the waves, surrounded by many people who had come to say goodbye. Before she swam away she told the people to come back to the same shore exactly one year later and they would see the cows arriving. Then she dipped below the waves and was never seen again.

The people waited for the year to pass and returned again to the edge of the Western Sea. They thronged the cliffs and the shoreline from early in the morning on the May eve. As the day broke and light filled the sky, they saw the three cows coming, just as the sea-maiden had told them – a white cow, a black cow and a red cow, all with sleek skin, large soft eyes and curved horns.

The cows stood on the shore for a time then moved towards the land, each going in a different direction. The black cow went south, the red cow went north and the white cow crossed the plain heading for Tara, the place of the high kings, in the centre of Ireland. There, she gave birth to twin calves: a male and a female.

Wherever they went, places were named after them and they were revered by the people.

To this day, cows are still highly prized in Ireland.


## GENEROSITY ABUSED

There was once a cow that would fill any container that was put under it. One day, it arrived at the house of an old woman who had no cow of her own. She was delighted when she saw it, as she was always begging her neighbours for milk they could spare for her.

She placed a vessel under the cow and was delighted when it was filled to the brim. The old woman brought out another container and it too was filled.

She knew the cow wouldn't fill the same container twice but that it would always release milk when a vessel was under it.

However, the good fortune of the cow's arrival at her house did not last, because the old woman turned her own luck. Greed and recklessness came over her and she began to put under the poor cow every container she could find. She collected milk in jugs and basins and every possible vessel imaginable, big and small. Then she placed a sieve under the cow and the milk poured endlessly through the holes, running over the countryside until it flowed like a white river.

The cow's generosity had been taken advantage of and the animal raced away to the nearest lake and threw itself in, never to be seen again.

When the old woman's neighbours found out what had happened, they were incensed, because she hadn't just lost the cow for her own needs but for everyone else's too. They killed her for being so wicked and for losing to the neighbourhood the precious cow.


## BÓ MÓR'S LAST MILKING

A man in north Leitrim had a cow which was known as Bó Mór. It was a mighty cow in all ways – big and strong and full of milk. Every day the cow fed on rich pasture a distance from the house of its owner. Every evening the cow drank from the same pool that formed on the roadside, fed by a mountain stream. Most nights the cow slept by the pool too.

In that area there was a greedy man who knew that the cow always had more milk in her than the farmer who owned her could use. He was jealous of this farmer's wealth and wished the cow could be his.

One night he put a vessel as big as a barrel under the cow and it filled to the top. The greedy man wanted even more than the first container-full but he knew the cow would fill any container only

once. So he knocked the bottom from a barrel, put it on top of the first vessel and managed to get his new, double-sized container right under the cow – she was tall enough for them to fit.

The greedy man laughed and laughed as he waited for the milk to pour into his huge makeshift tank. But he waited … and he waited … and nothing happened. The cow wouldn't give him another drop. And not only that, the cow kicked over the double container, spilling all the milk that had already gone into the first vessel.

And that cow, the beautiful, healthy Bó Mór, was never seen again in that place or anywhere else.

## A Knotty Curse Solved

A farmer and his wife had the finest herd of ten milking cows. Every year for three years running, the milk from the cows made so much delicious butter that the farmer's wife was in great demand at the market when she brought her produce. The couple were well off and delighted with the health of their cows.

But in the fourth year, no matter how well the farmer's wife churned the milk, it would not turn and the loss of their earnings from the butter made them poorer and poorer.

One day a stranger passed by and when he heard their sorry tale he told them that a curse must have been put on their yield.

He said that, since it was on a May morning that the butter was taken from them, they would have to wait until the following May to try to undo the curse.

The couple struggled through the rest of the year and into the following spring, eking out a living from what they grew on their land and the milk that wouldn't turn into butter.

When it came to May, they got up before dawn to see what would happen. As the sun came up, a woman they had never seen before entered the field and went from cow to cow. As she did so, she took a little drop of milk from each cow and tied a knot in a rope that she carried.

The couple watched the peculiar ritual, and when the stranger was bending down at the fifth cow the couple stood up and shouted at her to stop. They chased her and as she ran she dropped the rope in the field. Then she was gone from sight.

The man and his wife took the rope to the priest and asked him what to do. He told them to keep one knot and give each of the other four to their neighbours and that this would break the curse.

They did as they were instructed and went home, hoping that all would return to normal.

That day, they milked their cows and when they put it into the churn it turned perfectly and their beautiful butter was restored. In fact, it was so plentiful that they gained three times as much as they had lost.


## THE COW THAT WASN'T DEAD

A widow woman and her son who lived in south Leitrim had a cow that had just calved. One day, she woke to find the cow lying dead in the field and with great sadness she and her son dug a hole and buried the cow.

The woman had no other cows to nurse the calf but her neighbours were kind, taking turns to help hand-rear the calf and it soon became strong.

One morning, when the son was out early attending to the chores, he saw a cow coming towards the calf to let it suck her. As he watched the animal approach, he was certain it was their own cow, but how could it be, he wondered, if he and his mother had already buried it because it had died?

He watched it happen for several days to be sure and finally plucked up the courage to tell his mother, but she did not believe him. He watched again and was more than convinced, so this time he tried to persuade the priest. Once more, he was met with disbelief.

The young boy had no doubts that it was their old cow and he pestered the priest so much that eventually the priest told him what to do to try to prove it – or to forget about it altogether and accept that he was imagining things. The priest instructed him to get a bucket and fill it with milk then stir in some manure. He had to lie in wait early the next morning for the cow to appear again and, as soon as the calf had finished suckling from the cow, the boy must wind his hand around the cow's tail and hold onto the pot in the other hand. If it really was their cow, and it had been stolen by the fairy, it would probably head for the fairy fort on top of the hill. The boy had to have the courage to go all the way in there and do what he had to do to break the spell.

Next morning the boy did exactly as the priest had described – but only up to a point. He held on as well as he could but the cow was so strong he lost his grip and it ran off into the fairy fort. Now he was certain that the fairy were playing tricks on them and that this was their old cow, the mother of their own calf.

The next morning, the widow's son tried to hold on to the cow and failed again, even though this time he held his grip until the edge of the fairy fort.

The priest told him that if he failed a third time he and his mother would never get their cow back.

On the third morning, the young boy was determined not to let go of the cow, no matter how strongly she pulled away.

He was lying ready, long before the cow appeared. Once more, it came from the fairy fort and went into the field where the calf stood. As soon as it approached the calf, the young animal went straight to its mother for a drink. The young lad readied himself, making sure he had a good hold on the bucket of milk and manure, and stretched and tightened the fingers of his free hand to test his grip.

At last the calf began to move away, having drunk enough. The boy moved quickly, winding his hand a few times around the tail until he had a vice-like grip in the thickest part.

The cow tried to shake him off but he held on for his life. Up the hill towards the fairy fort they went, the boy holding on to the cow and to his bucket of milk and manure. This time he did not lose his grip. He held on as the cow went into the fort and there, within it, he saw fairy horsemen running around. He threw the contents of his pail over them and broke the spell that had kept his cow in their fort.

Without any problem from the fairy, the boy was able to calmly lead his cow back to the pasture and to her waiting calf.

His mother and the priest were delighted with the news that he had succeeded. Out of curiosity, they dug the hole where they had buried what they thought had been their cow and found in it only a stick.

From then on their cow was certainly fully alive and strong, and gave not only fine yields of milk but also healthy calves every year.

## Advice not Taken

A strange woman came past the farm of a man who was heading out on Garland Sunday, a day at the end of July for pilgrimage to holy sites and to honour the dead.

She offered to milk his cows while he and his family were away for the day. He didn't know who the woman was and he didn't trust her, fearing that she would put a spell on his cows.

As it turned out, his wife and children became sick soon after and all died. To the end of his days, the farmer regretted not trusting the person who made the offer, whom he was certain to have been a well-intentioned fairy woman.

## Poor, Rich, then Poor Again

On the shores of Lough Allen lived a family that had no cows and they were very poor. One day a large black cow appeared to come straight from the lake and head towards their house. The strange animal stood outside the front door and the woman of the house was certain that the cow wanted to be milked. The woman did so and the cow stayed in their field.

Time passed and from that day the family had not only a plentiful supply of milk but also an increasingly valuable herd of young calves, all from the same black cow.

When the farm was well stocked and the family were supplied well beyond their own needs in milk and butter, the man of the house told his wife that it would make sense to take some of the cattle to the market and make some money. And, with the black cow herself being quite elderly now, perhaps he should sell her too.

His wife wasn't so enamoured by the idea of selling the old cow, as she felt a sentimental attachment to it, never forgetting for a moment the day the creature came to them from the lake and lifted them from their poverty. But her husband talked her into the plan and they went outside to decide which of the cattle to take to the market.

As they talked, the couple noticed the cows beginning to gather together and walk away from their usual pasture near the house. They continued to walk down to the edge of the field where it

bordered on to the lake, and they walked right into the water, disappearing completely. They were never seen again.

But for the memory of the years of plenty, the family were as poor again as they ever had been before the day that the black cow came to their rescue.

## How Battlebridge Might Have Got its Name

There was once a farmer who lived on the well-known hill of Sheemore in the south of Leitrim. He had twenty cows, as well as other livestock, and was making a good living.

One evening, as he and his wife went about their usual chores, including the milking, they heard a child crying. They knew it wasn't one of theirs. At the same time, one of the cows kicked the bucket they were milking into, spilling its contents. The next evening, the same thing happened.

Now in those days stories about the fairies were common and the farmer had an idea what was going on – the fairy needed some milk from him for their own children.

He spoke into the air, addressing whoever might see him, even if he couldn't see them. He pointed to a cow, offering to the fairies that, if they needed it, they could help themselves to the milk of the one that had kicked over the pail of milk.

The farmer and his wife saw no one enter their fields but they knew that, every evening, that particular cow was being milked. This went on for about two years.

One day, the landlord and twenty soldiers turned up at the farm, demanding rent, and the farmer, though he was getting on well, did not have enough to pay what was being asked. The landlord allowed no time for negotiation and, as he insisted on immediate payment, he took away all of the farmer's animals, leaving him and his wife destitute.

The farmer went out into the fields and along the roads nearby and as he walked he spoke, just as he had done before, into the thin air, to whoever might be listening. He called on those he had helped and asked why, in the time of his own need, they hadn't helped him in the way that he had helped them so readily. No answer came and he went home, sad and forlorn.

At that moment the landlord and his men were just about to drive the cattle across a bridge that spanned the River Shannon. Suddenly, apparently from nowhere, a shower of sticks and stones began to fall on their heads. It was so severe that there was chaos as the land-lord and his men tried to protect themselves and ride for cover. As they did so, the cattle were turned around and driven back in the direction from which they had come. No matter what the landlord and his soldiers did to try to steer the cattle back the way they were meant to be going, the cattle seemed to have their own minds – or were helped by unseen hands – to head back towards Sheemore. The landlord and his soldiers were forced to give up their attempts and were more than glad to reach their homes in safety.

The farmer and his wife were delighted when they saw all their animals returning to the farm, and thanked their invisible helpers. They were left in peace to get on with their lives. It is said that this strange event is the reason that this particular bridge over the River Shannon is known as Battlebridge.


## A WORD IN JEST LOSES A COW

There was once an old woman and her son who lived near Lough Gill. Their living was meagre but they at least had one cow, which gave them their needs in milk and butter. To eke out their living, the old woman made besoms, or brooms, from the sturdy heather twigs and sold them at the market in Sligo town. It was the son's job to cut the heather for her when he took the cow to the hillside pastures to graze.

One particular day, he spent hours cutting the best heather branches he had seen in a while; he knew his mother would be delighted with his harvest. Before going home, he rested on the warm, comfortable heather and soon fell asleep.

When he woke he was amazed to see a crowd of fairies nearby, playing football. He watched in amazement and soon was so caught up in their game that he forgot himself and suddenly called out: 'Well done, red cap!' to one of the fairies who was wearing a bright red cap and who was particularly good at keeping the ball.

The minute he spoke, the football suddenly left the field of play and came flying through the air, hitting the lad square on the face and blinding him temporarily in one eye. He couldn't believe it. He had meant well when he had shouted his support to the red-capped player.

When he recovered from the smarting pain of the smack from the ball and could see clearly again, he looked around. All the fairies had gone – and so had his mother's precious cow.

Darkness was falling and he didn't want to get lost on the hill-side trying to find the cow, and he certainly did not want to fall into one of the many bog-holes that were impossible to see, so the only thing for it was to head for home.

Once home, he confessed to the story about why he had no cow walking beside him. Understandably, his mother was furious with him to lose their precious animal; it was their only cow after all. The cow had to be found and brought home.

Next day the two of them walked up the hill and called and called but they couldn't find her anywhere. Then, on the way down again, they spotted the cow, but all was not well. She was in a bog-hole and all that showed above ground were her horns. It was too much work for the two of them alone to try to rescue the poor animal, so they went down the hill again and asked all their neighbours to come and help.

At the bog-hole, ropes were tied around the cow's horns and she was pulled clear, but by the time her body surfaced fully it was clear that she was dead.

Now the old widow had only her besoms to bring in money for food and it was hard work for her and also for her son, who had to cut even more heather for her to make enough brooms.

One day, when he was hard at work on the hillside, he was certain he saw their cow again, with two small men watching over her. He called over, saying: 'That's my mother's cow!'

The men denied it so the lad went over to the cow and grabbed it by the horns, certain that it was their own cow and that, whatever had been found in the bog-hole, was not. It was more than likely to have been a trick by the fairy, who wanted the cow.

The lad was still holding on to the horns when the two strange men drove the cow to the very edge of the cliff and both the lad and the cow fell down into Lough Gill.

When they came up to the surface, the lad was confused to find himself standing in front of a fancy castle, which wasn't normally there at the lough side. He knew it must be a fairy castle.

A kingly-looking man came out of the castle and offered him enough gold to buy twenty cows, but the lad refused, saying the only thing he wanted was to get back to his mother with their one true cow.

He was offered more gold in bulging bags but still he refused it as he sensed it was a trick. But it didn't pay him to appear so ungrateful and before he could do anything to save himself, he was kicked and punched by the king's servants.

Then a strange gust of wind came and the lad and the cow were swept away from the castle and found themselves standing properly by Lough Gill again. The lad was relieved and couldn't believe his luck. He began the walk back to his house, happy to be bringing the cow home to his mother.

But the fairy weren't finished with him yet and close to the house another gust of wind came up, with swirling leaves blowing towards him and the cow. The lad knew this was a fairy wind and he tried to steer the cow away from where the gust was coming but the cow stood stock still.

The lad did the one thing left that he could think of – he blessed the animal, hoping that this would protect it. But it wasn't enough or in time. The cow disappeared into thin air, the strange wind stopped and all was calm, but of course, once again, the lad had to go into the house and tell his sorrowful mother all that had happened.

The old widow and her son lived in poverty to the end of their days and people say it was on account of the lad interfering with the fairy – perhaps a lesson that's best learned before the fact, not after it, as this lad found out to his cost.

## THE HARE AND THE OLD WOMAN

Old Hugh McNulty was sick and tired of the loss of his cows' first milking of the day. Each morning, for a month, he went into his byre expecting to get fresh milk for breakfast, but all of the cows would be dry.

He decided to find out the reason – he had his suspicions. One evening, he concealed himself in a corner of the barn and prepared to wait as long as it took. At midnight, a hare came into the byre and went from cow to cow, sucking each one until it groaned.

The farmer's suspicions were confirmed. He fired a shot at the hare and injured its leg. The hare escaped but could not run fast and Hugh was able to follow it over the fields until it turned into a lane below Conwall graveyard.

It entered a small house, jumping over a half door. Hugh McNulty wasted no time and went inside. There, sitting by the fire on a low stool, was an old woman tending a wound on her leg.

He had never seen her before and asked her name. She refused to give it but told him, 'Your cows are safe now, Hugh McNulty. Go home.'

From that day, the farmer was bothered no more and his cows gave him all the milk he needed.

# REFERENCES

The full text of Shae Clancy's article, 'Cattle in Early Ireland', can be viewed on: http://www.applewarrior.com/celticwell/ejournal/beltane/cattle_early_ireland.htm.

**The First Cows in Ireland:** various sources including NFCS197:112; Collector: Ita Gormley, Girls National School. Tamhnach Fhuinsineach School. Teacher: Seosamh Ó Reachtnáin.

**Generosity Abused:** based on story in NFCS189; Pat Gilroy, Farmer, 70, Pronghlish, Glenade. Gleann Éada School. Teacher: Bean Uí Mhaolaith.

**Bó Mór's Last Milking:** Based on story in NFCS193:81; Mrs Francis Rooney, Mullies, Manorhamilton, aged between 60 and 70. Gleann Éada School. Teacher: Bean Uí Mhaolaith.

**A Knotty Curse Solved:** NFCS199:31; Annie Byrne (pupil), Moneyduff.

**The Cow that Wasn't Dead:** Based on story in NFCS199:37; B Cunningham (75), Cartron, Fivemilebourne. Collector: Patrick Healy, Moneyduff NS, Dromahair. Teacher: Pádhraic Ó Heádhra.

**Advice not Taken:** NFCS201:259. Drumlease School. Teacher: Tomás Diolín.

**Poor, Rich, then Poor Again:** NFCS207:524; Michael Mulhair (75), Sramore. Collector: Rose McBrien, Cormongan school. Teacher: Seán MacAmhalghaidh.

**How Battlebridge Might Have Got its Name:** NFCS210:16; Michael Geoghan, Aughacashel. Collector: Michael Geoghan, An Mhainistir, Cara Droma Ruisc. Teacher: an Bráthair Eoghan.

**A Word in Jest Loses a Cow:** NFCS201:180; John Flynn, Kilcoosey. Collector: Annaleen O Neill, Drumlease School. Teacher: Tomás Diolín.

**The Hare and the Old Woman:** NFCS189:71; Pat Gilroy (70), farmer, Proughlish, Largydonnel. Glenade School.

# 8

# HUMOROUS TALES: DID I TELL YOU THE ONE ABOUT … ?

## THE PENNY TRICK THAT MADE TWENTY POUNDS

A young lad went to the fair to sell a cow and buy some goats. Soon people came to ask how much he wanted for the cow.

'The highest penny,' he replied.

Two or three farmers looked at each other then took their walking sticks and put a penny on top of each one, stretching the sticks high into the air.

Young Johnny made his bargain with the 'highest penny' and went home without his cow and certainly without goats.

The next day, the farmer who bought the young lad's cow felt bad about cheating him, presuming him to be foolish, so he decided to seek him out and give a better price for the cow. He found out where the lad lived and went to the house.

An old woman opened the door and told him he was probably too late to meet her son as he had just died. However, she said she had a magic stick that might just be able to bring him round, as he wasn't too long dead.

The farmer was saddened to hear the news but also intrigued to hear about the magic stick. He went into the cottage to watch her. She took a stick from the table, struck her son's head lightly and instantly he jumped up, appearing to be as well as ever.

The farmer was amazed and asked if the old woman would sell the stick to him.

'I'm not so sure. I wouldn't want to lose my son again and not be able to bring him back. I need him to work here,' she said.

Now, the old woman had no magic at all and the son had not been dead. They were not as foolish as the farmer had thought and had set up the trick at the fair.

The farmer, who was now the foolish one, was taken in by what he thought he had seen. He began to think of the ways he could make money from the stick, not least by trying to get a reward to treat a king who was very sickly and likely to die unless a cure was found.

He bargained with the old woman and eventually she agreed to part with it for £20 – enough to buy a whole herd of goats, and more besides.

The next day the farmer set out for the king's castle, and when he got there he told them he had a magic stick that could make sick people better and even bring people who had just died back to life.

He was ushered into the king's chamber where he immediately went over to the king and whacked him hard on the head with the stick. The king died instantly and the poor farmer was taken out and shot.

Meanwhile, Johnny and his mother lived well to the end of their days with one of the healthiest goat herds for miles around. They were no fools.


## A BET ON A LIFE

Many years ago, in the townland of Faughery, young Patsy put in a good day's work for his boss, old John. He rarely slackened from the back-breaking chores of pulling heavy stones from the land to improve it for tilling. He drove the cows for hours to find decent grass and when it came to work in the bog, he was second to none at the speed he could cut.

But as John got older and annoyed at being less able to do the farm work, he started to find fault with the way Patsy was working and soon he was picking arguments with him.

One day when John was pushing Patsy hard with his niggling, Patsy looked up from his digging and declared: 'I bet you your brand new litter of bonhams* that I can steal the sheet from your bed this very night!'

Old John glared at him. 'Take my best bonhams would you? They're worth a fortune. Anyway, you could never creep into my bedroom to do that. I'd soon catch you and if I didn't my wife is a light sleeper and she'd have you by the throat.'

The two rallied on and John laughed at the cheek of Patsy's bet. By evening time he told the young man: 'You're on, but I'll be ready for you, so don't think you have a hope of winning this bet. And if you lose, you'll lose your job as well.'

When it was dark, Patsy went off to the graveyard and raised the body of a man recently buried. He carried the corpse back to John's house and hauled it up on to the roof. Slowly he let the corpse down the chimney.

Old John was waiting by the fireplace, expecting that this would be how Patsy would try to get in. He had an axe in his hand and he struck a blow much harder than he intended, so much so that the body of what he thought was Patsy fell in a heap on the floor.

His wife called out and asked him what the clatter was. 'Everything's fine. I caught him right away and I'll get rid of him now. That's the last we'll see of him. He lost his bet.'

John took what he thought was Patsy's dead body and carried it down through the field where he planned to dig a grave for it in daylight.

While he was gone, Patsy went down the chimney and straight to the bedroom where John's wife was lying, half asleep.

'Ah move over a bit now, I'm cold,' he said to her.

John's wife was surprised that he would be back so soon. 'You weren't long burying the body,' she said.

'Never mind about that, just move over and make room for me,' urged Patsy.

As soon as she moved across the bed, Patsy got up and smartly pulled the sheet from under her and ran from the house.

When John came back he knew he had been tricked and that the beautiful litter of newborn bonhams would be Patsy's.

The next day Patsy came to conclude the bargain and pick up his prize. John had no choice but to part with the precious litter. With the money Patsy made from selling the creatures he was able to set himself up in business and be his own boss from that day on.

*bonham – from the Irish '*banbh*', meaning piglet

## The Man who had no Story

On a fine spring day, Johnny set off from his house near Mullagh to buy a new horse at the fair. He went over the mountains and made good progress until the darkness closed in around him suddenly. He realised he needed to find a place to stay the night.

He saw some lights not far from his path and stopped at the first house, asking if he could have a meal and a bed to sleep on. Johnny was welcomed in and after a hearty meal he sat with the family by the fire. His host asked if he had a story to tell but Johnny apologised and said he hadn't any. So the host suggested maybe a song then and again Johnny confessed he had no songs.

The family looked at each other in surprise at the reluctance of the visitor to share something to pass the time. The man of the house suggested his wife prepare the bed straight away, as their guest must be very tired if he had no energy to tell a story or sing a song.

What Johnny did not hear was the whisper by the man of the house into his wife's ear: 'He'll have a story by the time he leaves here.'

Johnny prepared to go to bed. He decided to be extra careful with the money he had in his coat to buy the horse, so he undressed fully then put on his waistcoat, with the money tucked into a deep pocket, and put his shirt on over that. He didn't want to be robbed in the middle of the night.

Now it happened that there was a wake in a house nearby and the man of the house told his wife: 'Go up to the bed and lie beside the visitor. I'll go to the wake now.'

She went into the bedroom where Johnny lay sleeping. Awakened by her arrival, Johnny turned round and saw it was the woman of the house.

'I'm sorry but this isn't right. You shouldn't be in my bed. What'll your husband think when he comes in? Please leave straight away!' he demanded.

She paid no heed and replied: 'Don't worry. He won't be back until morning.'

Moments later the man of the house came running into the bedroom with a pitchfork in his hand and shouted at poor Johnny: 'What's going on here? I give you the best of hospitality and a good dry bed for the night and you have the cheek to take my wife as well. Get out of here this minute!'

Johnny was in shock. Without stopping to dress, he ran down the stairs and out into the cold night. He had no idea where to go. He saw a light in a neighbouring house and ran straight into the wake that his host had talked about. He was shaking and shivering with the cold and the embarrassment.

The people at the wake were understandably alarmed but the family reassured them that everything was alright. The man of that house put an old coat around their startled guest and offered him a drink to calm his nerves.

As soon as Johnny was settled, though still confused by what had happened, the man of that house told him: 'My brother is a bit of a prankster. He likes to play tricks on people and obviously he picked on you this evening. I'm sure there's an explanation for why he did this.'

Johnny's host arrived at the wake house a little later and greeted Johnny with a hearty chuckle. 'Well now, my friend, I'm sure that you'll have a story to tell at the next house you visit! Come away back with me now and I'll give you a mug of tea to warm you up before you go back to bed.'

After seeing the man's grin and realising that he had indeed been the victim of a prank, Johnny eventually saw the funny side of it. After a good night's sleep and a fine breakfast he thanked his hosts for all of their mighty hospitality and assured them he would never forget his time with them. 'My friends will never believe me. They'll think I've made up this story, but, you're right, I have at least one story ready to tell folk the next time I'm asked.'


## A Very Clever Harper

There is a story about a harper from Drumshanbo called Jerome O'Duigenain who lived in the late eighteenth century and whose great musical skills won him a prize of 100 guineas.

In 1780, an English nobleman arrived in Dublin, accompanied by his Welsh harper. The visitor dared to make the boast that none could play the harp as well as his Welsh companion.

The challenge was taken up by Col Jones, a member of parliament for Leitrim who knew the fine skills of the Drumshanbo harper. He accepted the challenge from the Englishman and immediately sent a messenger to invite O'Duigenain to make the three-day, 150km ride to Dublin to prove his talent. He was invited to bring with him a suit of 'canthic' (a costume made from beaten rushes). With equal enthusiasm – and the prize of 100 guineas dangling in front of him – O'Duigenain agreed to the contest and set off for Dublin, cheered on his way by crowds of well-wishers. He was met by Col Jones outside the city gates and escorted in with great pomp and ceremony.

Tickets for the contest were so keenly sought-after that no hall large enough could be found, and the unusual and unprecedented step was taken to use the 'floor' of the then parliament building in College Green.

On the day of the contest, the room normally reserved for political debate was thronging with the nobility of the city and beyond. The first to play was the Welshman. There was no question that he was anything other than an excellent harper and Col Jones was a little uneasy about how the contest would bear out, but O'Duigenain waited quietly for his turn and then took to the floor. In his strange, perhaps comical, suit of rushes, he bowed solemnly at the empty Speaker's Chair and began his repertoire. The Leitrim harper played rousing tunes, joyful tunes, then laments, and at the end not a dry eye was left in the house. He bowed once more to the empty chair then took his seat beside Col Jones. There was wild applause and when all the cheering had died down he was declared the winner and given the enormous wager placed by the English visitor.

The story goes that he remained in Dublin fulfilling many invitations from the wealthy in their fine houses, playing at concerts and banquets. He earned much and finally turned for home, with many a fine tale to tell of his exploits in the capital and with all his tunes, including the ones which won him the accolade, more than able to cheer his delighted friends on his victorious return. When word came that he was on his way, bonfires were lit on the hills around Drumshanbo and he was welcomed as nothing less than a hero.

Tales of this event were kept alive and passed on by the folk of Drumshanbo and not least through the generations of O'Duigenains who continued to live in Drumshanbo well into the twentieth century.


## THE GOLDEN HORSE

Patrick worked at a big country house and was trusted by the estate owners. One day, he was asked to take a cow to the market to sell it and told to get the very best price available.

When he arrived at the market, he walked around for a while, looking at the other animals for sale and listening to the prices being discussed. He knew he needed to get as good a deal as the ones he heard being struck.

He haggled and bargained until he got a price that he knew would please his master and then set off on his journey home. It was late in the day and he realised he would need to stay the night somewhere in case he was robbed on the dark road.

He found an inn where he could get a meal and lodgings. What Patrick didn't know was that a robber had been watching him haggle and bargain at the market and knew exactly what the young lad had in his pocket. He had followed him on his horse and saw Patrick go into the inn, so he made a plan. It would be easy pickings.

The robber stayed at the inn too and was up at the crack of dawn ready to pounce on Patrick as he walked home. The robber watched to see what road Patrick took and soon afterwards he took his horse and rode out in the same direction.

On a quiet stretch of lane the robber circled beside Patrick and demanded to get the money. Patrick refused then realised he was no match for the determined robber, who was tall and very strong. Patrick took the money from his pocket, but instead of handing it over he threw it in the air and the notes were blown about.

'There you are then,' said Patrick. 'If you want it so badly you can pick it up. It's all yours.'

The robber bent down to gather up the notes and in an instant Patrick grabbed the reins of the horse and jumped on it, galloping away as smartly as possible, leaving the robber speechless.

Arriving back at his workplace, Patrick rode into the yard and dismounted. His master looked at him and asked: 'Did the cow turn into a horse?'

Patrick told him what had happened and described the rough-looking man who must have been spying on him at the market.

When Patrick took off the saddle to brush down the horse after the long, hard ride, he found bags of gold and silver hidden

underneath it. It was a lifetime's earnings for any man. His master insisted that it was all Patrick's for his quick-thinking when the robber attacked him.

Patrick was able to buy half his master's land with the unexpected treasure and set himself up in farming, at which he prospered, and in due course married one of his former master's daughters.

## The Tail that Wagged the Dog that Saved the Boy!

Young Tom was fed up of the drudgery of life, scraping out a meagre living from day to day. One morning, he packed a few things, wrapped them in a cloth and closed his door for the last time. He had decided to set off in search of his fortune.

At the end of his first day on the road, he inquired at a house for a meal and a bed and was invited in. There was only an old man there. He said he had two sons but they were out and wouldn't be back for a while.

When Tom had sat long enough after supper he excused himself and went to bed, but felt uneasy. He didn't feel he could trust the old man – Tom had noticed the old fellow had been very nervous when he spoke about his sons. So when Tom got into bed, he lay more awake than asleep and eventually he heard the door open and close when the sons returned.

He listened as they told their father that they had a bullock with them, which they had stolen. They cleaned the animal and clattered about, making a lot of noise. Finally, they told their father to go to the bed where Tom was lying and to lie beyond the visitor, at the wall. They would take care of Tom.

This didn't sound at all pleasant and when the old man came into the room and climbed over towards the wall beyond where Tom was lying, Tom was careful to remain as still as he could, breathing softly, pretending he was sound asleep.

He continued to lie quietly until he heard the old man snoring deeply. Carefully, he climbed over the sleeping old man and drew himself right up against the wall.

Soon he heard the sons coming up the stairs. They opened the door and stood beside the bed. They had a hatchet with them but no light, as they didn't want to disturb the visitor. In an instant Tom heard the ghastly sound of a blade cutting through flesh and he squirmed at the thought of what might have happened to him. But his life wasn't out of danger by a long shot. He still had to get out of the house and he had no idea what would happen next.

Having done the dirty business they had planned, the sons went out of the room carrying what they presumed was Tom's head. They took it straight to the garden and dropped it into a hole they had prepared, still not realising they had just killed their own father.

Tom climbed over the dead body of the old man. He had gone to bed fully dressed, due to his suspicions, so was downstairs in no time, while the sons were still out in the garden. He looked for another door or a window but saw no means of escape. He needed to find somewhere to hide since escape now was impossible.

From being in the room earlier, he remembered only the table and chairs and a couple of stools by the fire. Then he caught sight of an old wooden chest and lifted the lid to see how roomy it was. The bottom of it was thick with notes and coins. But it was a large, deep chest and there was just enough room for him to crouch into it and pull down the lid in the nick of time.

The sons stood in the doorway and Tom heard them tell their dog to lie by the open door and guard the house. They talked about burying the rest of the body in the morning and set off upstairs to their beds. One of the sons noticed that the chest wasn't locked and he went back downstairs to secure it with a padlock, much to Tom's dismay.

Once the sons were long gone to bed and the house was as quiet as it would ever be, Tom poked about inside the chest to try to find a way to escape. It was a sturdy box, made of thick, strong wood and he would not be able to burst through it.

Tom's fingers found two small holes, one on either side, probably for carrying the chest. He pushed his fingers through one hole, to see how far they would go. It was big enough for his whole hand.

He began to whistle to attract the dog's attention. It wasn't long before the dog growled at the strange noise coming from the trunk and got up to investigate. It walked around the trunk sniffing. Tom pulled in his hand so he could use the hole to see the size of the dog. It had a long, thick tail.

He began to whistle again and put out his hand as the dog prowled around the chest. As the dog passed, he caught the tail and held on to it firmly, which of course didn't charm the dog.

Now it began to snarl and pull, to try to release whatever was holding its tail. Tom hoped the sons wouldn't wake up too quickly.

The dog was so strong that the trunk started to move, which was exactly what Tom had hoped. It pulled and pulled and, thankfully for Tom, it headed straight for the open door, with the trunk bumping out of the house and over the path.

Tom remembered that the house was on a steep hillside and, as the dog ran on, the chest gained speed. Tom decided to take a chance and let go of the dog's tail. The chest rolled over and over, down the hill and finally burst open. Beaten and bruised, Tom was free, not minding his bashing as it was a lot better than losing his head.

He went over to where the remains of the chest lay and he found plenty of the notes and coins lying around and under it. He gathered up as much as he could and stuffed it in his pockets. Not sure of his bearings, and in too much shock to try to make his way immediately, he walked a short distance until he found a small clump of trees where he could hide and wait until daylight.

When the first light of morning came, Tom got up. He needed to be well out of the way before the sons found out their terrible mistake. He was stiff and sore, covered in cuts and bruises. He carefully found his way down the hill and back on to the track that led him far from the ordeal of the night before.

However, the route Tom chose that morning was not into the big wide world of adventure and finding his fortune. He took the shortest road that led straight back to his own front door. He had had enough adventure for one lifetime and, with the small fortune he had taken from the trunk, he was content to stay at home for the rest of his days where he felt safe.

After all, he reflected, what was a bit of hard work to grow your own food and look after a few animals, compared to the risk of the unknown world where an innocently-intended adventure could end up in losing his life.

## An Unusual Self-Portrait

A man who lived far from places where anything other than food and basic everyday items were sold was once on a trip to a big town. He entered a shop selling fancy furniture, linen and clothes.

He saw a small mirror on a wall but, having never seen one before, didn't know this was what it was.

He looked at it directly and was amazed to see the familiar features of an old man looking back at him – none other than his father, he thought. Amazed, he bought the item and took it home. He didn't show it to his wife. Instead, he would take it out of his pocket and look at it when he thought his wife wasn't noticing. Of course, she did notice but didn't say anything, wondering to herself what he might have in his pocket that he needed to keep secret.

One day her husband went out without his coat and she went straight to the coat and took out the item, not knowing it was a mirror. Having never seen one before either, she looked directly in it and saw the wrinkled, time-worn face of an old woman looking back at her. Not realising she was looking at a reflection of herself, she put the 'picture', as she thought it to be, back into her husband's coat and sighed. 'Well,' she said to herself, 'if that is the old one he is after, he can have her.'

## THE YOUNG GREY MARE

For many years, several locations at Mohill were used for horse races, which attracted great crowds. On the outskirts of the town is a field still known as 'race park'. Another area, on a large farm at Tullybradan Hill, was attractive because it had one of the flattest and largest fields in the vicinity. Around the Mohill area there are still many people with life-long interests in horses, in particular with the Irish Draught horses, the national horse breed of Ireland. Originally developed for farm work, the breed is now used for crossing with thoroughbreds and warmbloods to produce Irish Sport horses, which excel at the highest levels of show jumping and eventing.

In many parts of the Irish Folklore Collection schools archive, I came across a poem about a horse which obviously became a legend in its own lifetime. I tried to find a living source for it and it was clear that everyone I talked to had heard about 'Lynch's mare', sometimes known as the 'flying white mare', but no one could recite the poem to me. I am grateful for the permission of UCD to use a version of the poem included in the schools collection.

You bards and muses who ne'er refuses
I hope your talent with me you'll share
While I endeavour with ardent labour
To sound the praises of the young grey mare.

She first was taken to the Mohill races
There was entered for the first prize
Where gallant sportsmen from every quarter
Gave down their names to be advertised.

Eleven o'clock was the hour precisely
At which the horses were set to run
They then were called to the place of starting
And off they went as the bell was rung.

Off they started but quickly parted
Like the start of Egypt she led them on
But on their return there was cause to mourn
For out of five there came in but one.

A mute disorder in every corner
Bespoke the envy of the betting men
Although the judges gave her no justice
In spite of all she the prize did win.

There was old Taylor and likewise Murphy
The next came Dolan from Ballinamore
Each of those men would bet possessions
To bring the prize from the other four.

At their conversation I grew impatient
To see one heat of the race put in
But in speaking fairly I grew enerwed?
When I saw Paul Davis down from Elphin.

He was rejected in Curragh Races
For lifting prizes in everywhere
But now his credit is forever broken
Since he came in contact with the Young Grey Mare.

He was rejected in the Curragh Races
'Twas said by magic that his horse could fly
They told me plainly I should not enter
For no horse in Europe could pass him by.

In twelve months after he went to London
And won a prize of ten hundred pounds
So Paul Davis never met his master
Till he came on the Mohill grounds.

There were six stewards and a judge appointed
To give justice to every man
Buyt like King Herod or Pontius Pilate
They condemned the just and set free the wrong.

There is one of them now must be exempted
Davis, noble he is called by name
As for the others in future ages
They should get scandal and public shame.

You solitary critics excuse my ramblings
On the observation I introduce
I have much trespassed on your attention
And again I beg to be excused.

Our valiant jockeys they now got warning
They had one moment to prepare
The bell was rung and off they started
Soon leading all came the Young Grey Mare.

My view was broken all in one moment
I grew uneasy to know who would win
When cheers re-echoed all through the racecourse
Saying clear the way boys, the Grey comes in.

Full twenty perches she kept clear before them
In awful speed she passed them by
Joyous hearts I bestow a thousand
Hurrah for Lynch it was all the cry.

It was advertised in all directions
The best of three heats the prize did win
The first and second she won quite easily
Just like an arrow she twice came in.

She was a credit to her noble jockey
No fall or stumble on her might fear
She was like a greyhound before the cur-dog
When in pursuit of that timid hare.

The red-mouthed judges being bribed
By Mr Davis down from Elphin
Said his jockey for riding falsely
Should loose the prize or go out again.

To show them plainly he was well able
Again he entered the starting ring
Which sailed a blemish on Mr Davis
And sent him crying home to Elphin.

Now proud Roscommon may boast no longer
I defy all Connacht to compare
Or one to equal the pride of Leitrim
I mean Miss Lynch or the Young Grey Mare.


## THE LONG AND THE SHORT OF IT

The night before his wedding a young man took out the parcel containing the new suit he had ordered. He tried it on and was amazed to discover that the trousers were several centimetres too long.

He asked his mother if she had time to cut off the extra length and sew a new hem, but she had her hands full with baking and cleaning in preparation for relatives coming for the wedding.

He tried to persuade his older sister, but she too had many tasks to finish before morning and she was unable to take on one more.

The groom-to-be asked his younger sister if she could try, but she too had more than enough to occupy her.

He decided the trousers would have to stay as they were and hopefully his wife-to-be wouldn't be too annoyed at their wedding the next day. She could adjust them after the wedding, he was certain.

The whole family went to bed late, after the house was cleaned and all the baking and preparations were complete – except of course the shortening of the groom's trousers.

One by one they woke up and each felt guilty for not having agreed to do the work. In turn, they went downstairs, measured off the extra length as they remembered it, sewed a new hem and went back to bed feeling satisfied. Each time, they put the trousers back into the parcel, so none of them realised what had been done when they took their turn.

In the morning, when the young man was getting dressed he let out a scream. His mother and sisters went running to see what was wrong. The trousers were all the way up to his knees. He certainly couldn't turn up for his own wedding with short trousers!

The whole family burst out laughing when they realised that their kind deed done in secret had backfired. One of his sisters ran to neighbouring houses and asked for the loan of a pair of trousers suitable for a man to stand up in for his own wedding. A pair was duly found and the young groom was able to stand confidently at the altar to wait for his bride.

## DEAL OR NO DEAL?

*The final story in this section is taken directly as it was found in the schools collection, with permission from UCD. It's an ingenious way to teach measurement.*

There lived a man in the townland of Tullycreve named James Kelly. One time, he went to the fair of the Black with two heifers, a black one and a white one. A jobber came up to him and asked how much for the black one along with the white one and poor James thought it was only one heifer that the jobber wanted so he said nine pounds. The jobber took hold of the two and gave James nine pounds for the two heifers.

When James went home to his wife that evening, he held his head down in shame and his wife was furious when she heard the story.

Twelve months later he went back to the same fair, again with two heifers, one black and one white. The same jobber came up and asked the same question: how much for the black one along with the white one?

Poor Kelly thought, and said, 'one blade of corn and give me leave to double it for half an hour.' The jobber did so and Kelly said he would have the policemen at the bargain and a half-crown of earnest. The jobber agreed to this.

The policemen were got and the bargain went on. This is the way he doubled the blade of corn:

A blade and a blade two, two and two four, four and four eight, eight and eight sixteen, sixteen and sixteen thirty-two, thirty-two blades a pinch.

A pinch and a pinch two, two and two four, four and four eight, eight and eight sixteen, sixteen and sixteen thirty-two, thirty-two pinches a fistful.

A fistful and a fistful two, two and two four, four and four eight, eight and eight sixteen, sixteen and sixteen thirty-two, thirty-two fistfuls a sheaf.

A sheaf and a sheaf two, two and two four, four and four eight, eight and eight sixteen, sixteen and sixteen thirty-two, thirty-two sheaves a stook.

A stook and a stook two, two and two four, four and four eight, eight and eight sixteen, sixteen and sixteen thirty-two stooks a stack.

A stack and a stack two, two and two four, four and four eight, eight and eight sixteen, sixteen and sixteen thirty-two, thirty-two stacks a haggard full.

A haggard and a haggard two, two and two four, four and four eight, eight and eight sixteen, sixteen and sixteen thirty-two haggard a townland.

A townland and a townland two, two and two four, four and four eight, eight and eight sixteen, sixteen and sixteen thirty-two, thirty-two townlands a barony.

A barony and a barony two, two and two four, four and four eight, eight and eight sixteen, sixteen and sixteen thirty-two, thirty-two counties of Ireland.

Kelly then said he would have the corn of England, Ireland and Scotland before the half hour is up.

The police begged him to stop or he would have the jobber robbed. The jobber had to settle with him and he had to give Kelly forty pounds.

Kelly took the money and the heifers home with him and said he was well paid for the one he was not paid for last year.

He arrived home and, hugging his wife, said, 'You thought I was a fool this day twelve months ago but am I not a smart man today?'

## REFERENCES

**The Penny Trick that made Twenty Pounds:** NFCS191:117; Gerard Haran, Bomahis, Buckode, shanachie, 76. Buckode School. **A Bet on a Life:** NFCS194:20. Caisleán Míle School. Teacher: M Ó Loingsigh.

**The Man who had no Story:** NFCS199:32; Hugh McSharry, 56, Mullagh, Dromahair. Collector: Maureen McSharry, Moneyduff NS, Dromahair. Teacher: Pádhraic Ó Heádhra.

**A Very Clever Harper:** NFCS207:91; Michael McManus, Murhaun, Drumshanbo. Collector: Sarah McManus, Drumshanbo (C). Teacher: Margaret Flynn. Also an anonymous printed article.

**The Golden Horse:** NFCS189:76. Diffreen School.

**The Tail that Wagged the Dog that Saved the Boy:** NFCS193:221. Gleann An Chairthe School, Killasnett. Teacher: Seán MagUalghairg.

**An Unusual Self-Portrait:** NFCS189:153. Collector: Molly MacTernan, Diffreen School.

**The Young Grey Mare:** Told in full with permission from UCD. NFCS209:34. An Clochar, Cara Droma Ruisc. Teacher: Ant Sr Emerentia.

**The Long and the Short of it:** NFCS199:24; Mrs Ellen Fowley (42), Kilmore, Fivemilebourne. Collector: John Fowley, Moneyduff NS, Dromahair. Teacher: Pádhraic Ó Heádhra.

**Deal or no Deal?:** Told in full with permission from UCD. NCFS195:471. Mhine Mór School. Teacher: Liam Ó Briain.

9

# GOOD MAGIC, BAD MAGIC, SHAPE-SHIFTERS AND TRICKERY

The selection of stories in this chapter is of the 'take this with a pinch of salt' variety – exaggerated events, questionable and quirky characters, some having to get the better of another to save their own lives. Like all good folk tales, the events described in these stories could have happened, could be true, or might fit simply into the category of a good yarn with which to pass the time of day.

The first, reproduced with permission in its original wording from the UCD schools collection, concerns the less bright son of a north Leitrim chieftain, who is reluctantly given to a sly sorcerer for a year to try to turn him into something a bit cleverer.

## TOM FEELY'S SON

Long ago, before the advent of Christianity, there lived in Glenade a chieftain named Tom Feely. He owned the greater portion of the glen, consequently he was very wealthy.

His family consisted of one son who was very easy going and did not reach the standard of cleverness his parents wished. The fact of the son's stupidity gave rise to a great deal of anxiety and Mrs Feely one day said to Tom that they should take him on a visit to a friend in Tullaghan, a place at the extreme end of County Leitrim, as this visit might improve his education.

As they were walking along the seashore they saw a man, who was a stranger to Tom and his son, land off a boat. He spoke to Tom and asked him if the boy with him was his son. Tom replied that he was but that he was not what his wife or he would like him to be as he was rather stupid. The man said that if they would give him the child he would keep him for a year and then take him back one of the cleverest men in Glenade.

When Tom told his wife this, she was in deep distress at the thought of parting with her only child, but she had only to wait patiently for the year to elapse. At the end of the prescribed time Tom again visited Tullaghan. When he reached the seashore the same man came in the boat and his son with him. But what seemed very strange to him was that his son did not speak. The man then

said to Tom that he promised to bring back his son but that he did not promise to give him to him. Turning the boat, he then rowed away from the shore.

Tom was grieved and would not go home to his wife without their son. Seeing a small boat nearby, he boarded it and went in pursuit of his son and after a time he reached an island. He looked round and saw his son coming towards him. The son said to his father that if he did as he told him he would succeed in his efforts to get him away. He told his father to sit at dinner when asked, cut the meat with his knife, take it on the fork, replace it on the plate and say that he would not eat until he got his son. A bag of wheat would be thrown on the floor and a number of pigeons would fly down and eat it. By looking closely at them he would notice a feather of one of the pigeon's wings raised up. This pigeon was his son.

When dinner was over he found the pigeon after a careful search and brought it home with him. The parents found that he had become a very clever boy.

One day he went to the races and he changed himself into a horse and won all the races. He told his father that gentry from all parts would be there and would strive to buy him but on no account to sell the bridle.

Everything happened as the son stated and when the bargain was complete Tom took the bridle off the horse and on returning home his son was there before him. He attended all races after that with a like result.

One day they flattered poor Tom in such a way that he forgot the bridle and went home without his son. The son was taken back to the island and for punishment left standing in a door with boiling oil pouring down on him.

One day he asked a man to throw three buckets of water on him and as he did so the spell was broken and Tom's son made his escape. They went in pursuit of him.

He turned himself into a fish and although his followers changed themselves into sharks he landed safely on land.

When on land, he turned himself into a hare and his followers gave chase in the form of hounds.

Near the river Duff he changed himself into a field of corn. They cut the corn and thrashed it. The particular grain in which he was hidden rolled into the river and nothing remained of the corn but the chaff.

In the river he turned into a trout and his followers changed themselves into salmon and went in pursuit of him.

At Muckrum they closed in on him but getting out of the river he turned into a hawk and his followers followed him in the form of eagles.

When he reached Loughmarron they were about to capture him. He turned towards his own home and got there in safety.

From that day to this the hawk is able to beat the eagle in the air.


## THE FIDDLER AND THE FAIRIES

There was once a popular fiddler called Pádraig, who was much in demand to play at céilí all over Leitrim and the neighbouring counties. He would sometimes stay at one house for several weeks, entertaining all who passed through, before moving on to his next engagement. Off he went, fiddle in hand, ready to begin again.

A fellow once came from near Manorhamilton to where the fiddler was playing in Glenade and asked him to play at a wedding that was about to happen. It was a long way to go, and all the more so since Pádraig was a bit under the weather and had a bad cold. But the man from the wedding party was persuasive and the fiddler agreed to go.

The trek was long and Pádraig was relieved when they arrived at the wedding house – and so were the guests, who were ready for the music to begin.

Three nights and three days of dancing and eating and drinking later, with many of the guests still asking for more, Pádraig excused himself as he had another céilí to play at in another part of the county.

It was early evening when he left to begin his journey to Manorhamilton over the rough paths through the mountains. A mist came down and of course the poor man became disorientated and lost his way completely.

He sat down by a rock, unsure what to do. After a while, the mist began to clear, showing a fairly full moon which shone over the mound of a fairy fort not far away. Suddenly, lively music filled the air and a door opened in the hillside. A host of fairy folk came tripping out, followed by their own fairy fiddler. The faster he played, the faster the fairy people danced.

It was all Pádraig could do to hold on to his own fiddle and try not to join in, as he wasn't certain if the fairy would like to be interrupted by a human musician – he had heard plenty of stories about the curses that were put on people for doing that, especially if their playing wasn't to the liking of the fairy.

But the lure of the tunes – many of which Pádraig knew – was too much and he just had to join in. He played note for note the same tunes that the fairy fiddler played and became so caught up in the joy of the music that he didn't notice the fairy fiddler stopping and the entire band of fairy standing around him in a circle. Their silver lances were pointing directly at him and it was only when he paused between tunes, waiting for a new one to begin – and of course it didn't – that he realised what was happening.

Pádraig was marched over to where the king and queen of the fairy host were sitting. The king had a golden wand in his hand and he touched Pádraig with it three times. Then he asked Pádraig the very questions which the fiddler feared – why was he there, who gave him permission to be there and, particularly, who gave him the right to steal tunes from them?

Pádraig pleaded with them that this wasn't his intent at all, far from it, and that he had lost his way in the mist. As a good fiddler himself, he was delighted to hear their wonderful music and had hoped it was alright to join in.

The fairy king told Pádraig that it would not be lucky for a mortal man to play three times any of the tunes he had heard that night. He could play any of them twice, but no more, and if he did it would be the last tune he would ever play.

Pádraig suddenly found himself standing alone on the hillside, not a fairy in sight nor a note of music in the air. It felt peculiarly quiet, and all the more so because the sky darkened and then a strange wind came, and it seemed to Pádraig that he was being lifted into the air and carried off the hillside. Before he knew it, he was on the ground again, the wind disappeared and the sky cleared under the bright moon. The slightly disconcerted fiddler found himself on the outskirts of Manorhamilton and he spared no time in seeking out the house of the friends he had been hoping to visit. He said nothing of his strange experience and certainly made no mention of the threat from the king of the fairy.

As ever, all of his tunes were in great demand. He played many and found himself playing one of the new tunes he'd learned from the fairy fiddler. His friends loved it and asked him to play it again, which he did. Later in the evening they asked for it again but he refused, offering any other tune but that one. Pádraig wasn't the kind of fiddler to refuse a request and the word soon got out that he had a new tune but that he was reluctant to let it be heard.

He had now made a rod for his own back. Everywhere he played from then on, people tried their best to persuade him to play his new tune, but he refused with all kinds of excuses.

Time passed and Pádraig continued to be in great demand. He made sure to learn many new tunes from fiddlers from up and down the country to try to put off the questions about the tune that he should never have played and wished he had never heard.

But at a wedding in Fermanagh, when the craic was good and the poteen was flowing, Pádraig had one too many to drink and he let his resolve slip. He began to play the tune, for the third time. He suddenly felt ill and the wedding guests became alarmed for him. He couldn't stop the tune and, just as the fairy king had warned, before the tune was finished he fell off his chair and was stone dead.

## The Fairy Pipers

In the north of Leitrim, near Benbo mountain, lived a mother and her two children. One sunny day, when the children were resting in the heather, they heard the beautiful singing of a thrush. When the singing stopped, the children clapped and thanked her for her enchanting song. However, they didn't expect to hear the thrush reply to them. She told them to sit up after sunset and watch for the nine fairy pipers who would come from the mountain playing music far nicer than any bird or human could play.

Next day, the children sat out again in the same place and waited until the sun went down. Just at that moment, a door opened in the mountain and a troop of nine pipers came out and began to play. They walked across the mountain and disappeared from view, although the children could still hear the enchanting music.

The children were speechless until the pipers were gone and then they rushed home to tell their mother all that they had witnessed.

In the following days and weeks the children kept their eyes on the spot on the mountain where the fairy pipers had emerged, but they saw nothing. When they tried to see the 'door' that they had been sure to see open, there was only a big rock.

## The Strange Beetle

There were two brothers who lived and farmed next door to each other. They grew oats, potatoes and vegetables enough for their families and animals. Most years, both had healthy harvests from their grain crops, but one summer, one of the brothers noticed that his green field of growing corn was becoming patchy. It couldn't be the weather flattening it or cattle straying into the field. The stalks of young corn were disappearing from the ground. The farmer was concerned about what was coming into his field and taking away his crop, so he decided to watch one night to try to find the answer. He crouched down in a corner of the field and waited until after dark. He was amazed to see a black beetle scurrying from stalk to stalk, digging them out of the ground at the root and carrying away a few at a time, transplanting them in the field next door that belonged to his brother! When the beetle returned for some more stalks, the farmer had a bag ready and he caught the creature.

Next morning, his nephew was walking around along the edge of the field examining the ground, as if looking for something. The farmer asked him what he was doing and the strange answer was that he was looking for his mother. Now the uncle knew who was in the bag. He opened it and the beetle flew out, going straight to the house next door, where she turned back into her human form. From that day on, no more stalks of corn went missing and both brothers got on with their work without disturbing the other's farm.

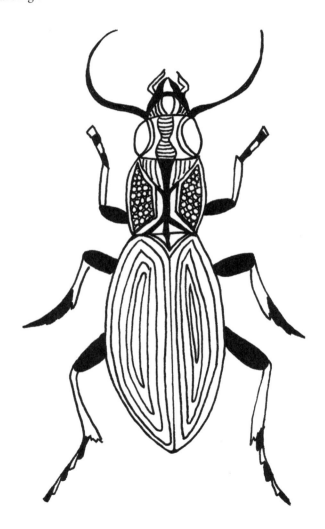

# STONE DEAF

*This story is expanded from a few small fragments of tales that explore the idea of what happens when we cross the boundary between the earthly and the otherworldly.*

Old Paddy Rooney was rumoured to have the best hearing on his townland in the Gurteen Mountains, and people were mindful of that. He could hear whispering from three fields away and when the subject matter concerned him, his hearing was even sharper.

Paddy was a fine farmer, he looked after his cows and always had healthy yields of milk. His vegetables grew well and he was able to look after affairs in his house too, keeping his small cabin clean and fresh without help from anyone, living alone as he did without wife or child. He baked bread and cakes, made soups and stews, and always had plenty to share.

Folk wondered why Paddy had never married. Rumours abounded about him being jilted by the women he proposed to, but no women confessed to refusing a proposal from Paddy. In fact, many eligible women in his glen would have been delighted to have said yes. So, clearly, that wasn't the reason.

There were others who said he'd been cursed by the fairy folk when he was a child and that he wouldn't be able to bear children. But no one could be sure of that one either, mainly because no one dared to ask him. Perhaps he was simply a contented bachelor.

As time went on, people couldn't remember much about Paddy's young days or the family he grew up in, except that, for all there was to recall, his had been as ordinary a family as any other. If he had had brothers and sisters, they were long gone and Paddy made no mention of them.

He wasn't so much a loner as a man who kept his own counsel, and he was more inclined to visit other folk down the valley than to invite too many to his fireside. His visits were few and far between and he listened more than talked, no matter how people tried to find a way to get him to talk about his life.

His seemingly lonely life went on unhindered from day to day, season to season, until the day that Paddy became ill and took to his bed. Nobody noticed anything wrong immediately, since Paddy's trips away from home were rare, so he wasn't missed immediately. But when folk down the hill noticed that smoke hadn't come from Paddy's chimney for several days and that his cows were making an unholy groaning sound with the discomfort of bulging udders, neighbours decided something had to be done.

A few farmers crept up to his house and pressed their noses against the window pane. Even though it was the middle of the day, it was dark as night inside and they could see nothing. They listened for a while and heard a pleading voice.

'Don't take me, not yet, I'm only sixty. You said I would live a long life even though you took away my chance of having a wife and children.'

It was surely Paddy speaking but who was he talking to, the neighbours wondered.

A rough, cold voice, like stone rubbing on stone, spoke: 'Paddy Rooney, I told you the day you threw stones down into my house in the cave that I would come for you when I was ready. Well, I am ready now. I'm lonely down there and I want you for company. My bones are creaking and gnarled with age and hard work. I need your strength to help me carry fuel for my fire and bale the water out of my cave. It fills quickly when it rains – and it rains plenty on these mountains – and I have to shift my belongings out of the way. I'm an old woman now and I can't manage on my own. My children have gone about their business and I can no longer fend for myself so I have come to take you with me.'

'How was I to know that the few stones I threw into the hole at Teampaill Teirhric to hear them rattle against the rocks were disturbing you? I didn't know you lived in that hole in the ground. Who would? I was just messing like any gossan*,' Paddy's hoarse voice groaned. 'You already made me half deaf when you slapped me on the side of the head and you cursed me further by stopping me from fathering children, just because I accidentally scared one of yours.

'Haven't I suffered for my whole life because of what that punishment meant, to be alone without wife or children? No-one understands why I haven't married. How can I tell them what happened? They'd laugh in my face.

'Why are you asking for more from me? Leave me in peace. I owe you nothing. I've lived the best life I can and I want to go on living it in my own house, looking after my animals and staying out of your way.'

The neighbours looked at each other in shock. What was that place they heard mentioned – Teampaill Teirhric? Surely, that was the strange deep fissure in the rocks that was a favourite of all the local gossans. Passing by on their way to the bog, it was a common pastime to compete to make the loudest clang by sending small stones rattling down the sides. No one knew how deep it was, but who would have imagined that someone lived down there? It couldn't be true.

No sounds came for many minutes and the neighbours wondered what to do. They had heard many a story about fairy curses and they knew full well that the fairy usually got the best side of any bargain they made. Dare they rush in and interfere? Could they do anything to help Paddy? They were frightened to risk their own lives, let alone Paddy's, if they did the wrong thing. They remained at the window in silence, trembling with fear that they would be caught.

They heard Paddy's weak voice again: 'I have a proposal. I will come for half of every week to help you out. I will give you half of the milk from my cows and of the makings of butter. I'll give you oats and vegetables. Is it enough? Will you leave me alone at that, to live out the rest of my years in peace?'

Silence again. Then they heard the cold, stony tones of the old woman from the cave – even though they still could not see her in the gloomy cottage.

'You drive a hard bargain, Paddy Rooney but your offer is fair enough. You can help me half the week at Teampaill Teirhric and give me half of everything from your produce. If you slip once, I won't waste time coming for you. I'll send the cold wind of death to take you from this world to mine in an instant. There will be no more bargaining. Goodbye Paddy Rooney but you'll be visiting me in my cave deep in the mountains soon enough. Don't forget your promise.'

'I'll keep it, don't concern yourself, old hag,' Paddy groaned from his bed.

The neighbours crept round the back of the house and hid under bushes. They waited to hear the door open and close but heard nothing. Suddenly, above their heads, a red-haired woman, with clothes the colour of dark storm clouds, flew out of the chimney and, in a strange, cold gust of wind that came from nowhere natural, she flew down the hill and disappeared out of sight, far below them, into the ground.

The neighbours stayed frozen to the spot until they were certain the strange visitor had gone. They crept around to the front of the house again and knocked on Paddy's door. A dull, weak voice called to them to enter and they did so nervously.

Paddy was lying on his bed in a pool of cold sweat with the covers thrown off him. He looked wan and much older than his sixty years, for he was a strong and healthy man, lithe and fit from all his work on the land.

His house was damp from days without fires and the neighbours shivered from more than the chill that they felt in his house.

They said nothing about what they had seen or heard and simply explained that the reason for their visit was to inquire about his health, as they hadn't seen smoke from his chimney in days and his cows had been heard groaning. They made no reference to the extraordinary scene they had just witnessed. Equally, Paddy told them nothing of the visitor, even though, when he raised himself up from his bed to speak, his voice seemed sadder than usual: 'I'm sorry, friends. I'm not in the best of health this week. Something laid me really low and I had no energy to get up. Are my cows all right?'

Joey O'Rourke, one of the neighbours, said: 'There's nothing that can't be sorted with a good milking. We'll do that for you straight away. And we'll go back to our own houses and get you some soup and bread to help you get back on your feet. You'll be standing strong on your own bones in a day or two.'

The farmers looked after Paddy over the next few days, with their wives and children helping out in every way they could. Paddy didn't resist. He appreciated their kindness and welcomed them into his home.

The neighbours who had witnessed the red-haired hag's visit swore to keep secret what they had seen, as there was nothing to gain by letting the story be known and passed on from busybody to busybody in their district and beyond.

However, on the excuse of Paddy's sudden illness, they looked for ways to help out in whatever way they could, since Paddy had to work twice as hard on his own farm to make up for the time he had to give up to help the old hag each week.

From that day on, people didn't whisper about why Paddy was a single man with no wife or children, nor did they try to guess if he'd been cursed by a fairy.

The farmers who kept their secret also made sure that no unkind words were said about him and, for fear of the curses that might easily have fallen on their lives when, as young gossans, they had thrown stones for fun into Teampaill Teirhric, they did everything they could to look out for their neighbour to the end of his natural days.

And of all they witnessed that day at Paddy's door, they might as well have been stone deaf themselves, for they kept the silence that they promised each other – except on rare occasions, when dark storm clouds crossed the sky and wild winds blew and they remembered that strange event. And in the dark of those nights, sitting close by the fire with their loved ones, they would whisper this tale and swear the listeners to the same kind of secrecy.

With Paddy and all his neighbours now long-since gone, I think it's all right for me to tell you this tale today. But be careful, though, the next time you pass a deep hole in the ground. Don't be tempted to go throwing stones, whether you're a gossan or a grown up. You don't want to meet the old red-haired hag or have to bargain with her for your life.

*gossan – young boy

## THE PERFECT HOSTESS

Three brothers called O'Leary were travelling tinsmiths who were regular visitors to the farms around Kiltyclogher, where their wares were always appreciated.

Once, not able to find lodgings in the district, they set off for Dowra and took a short cut over the mountains. A mist closed in on them and they lost their way. While they wandered around they saw a faint light and decided to make for it, hoping it to be a house where they could safely rest for the night, at least, and until the mist cleared.

As they got closer their confidence of hospitality and a warm bed grew, as the night was cold and damp and they wanted to be indoors.

They knocked on the door but no one answered. Surprised, they pushed open the door and saw a fine fire blazing away and a full meal cooking on it. The table was set with fine crockery. They called out and still no one came.

It made no sense to the O'Leary brothers, but such was their hunger that they ignored their manners and tucked into the hot, tasty dinner. They ate their fill, still the only ones in the house. It seemed a waste not to eat it.

They tidied up and decided to explore the rest of the house. They found a bedroom with three beds in it, and on each bed was a new suit of clothes and a pair of polished boots.

Soon, all three brothers were sound asleep and nothing disturbed their rest. When they rose in the morning, fresh from the best sleep they had had in months, they couldn't believe that an ample breakfast was waiting for them on the fire and yet they had heard no sounds in the night.

Once again, their enthusiasm to enjoy what seemed like perfect hospitality over-ruled waiting for their unseen host to turn up. They ate well, and even though the mist had cleared they were inclined to stay around and wait for the owner of the house to return.

Days passed. Weeks passed. Winter came and went. Six months passed and each day and night food and clothes were supplied, as much as they needed, but still they saw no one to thank for the unbelievable and unusual hospitality. In the barn stood a cow that gave the finest of milk and three horses that occasionally the men rode around on, without venturing too far from their peculiar lodgings.

But when the spring came and the warm sun beckoned them to travel the well-known lanes of north Leitrim and meet their friends at the local fairs, the three brothers grew restless, for even fine food and clothes are not sufficient to occupy active minds and hearts that enjoy the company of others.

The men set off on the three fine horses, heading for Drumkeeran fair. They hadn't ridden far when they were overtaken by a woman with a crown on her head and golden shoes on her feet.

She asked them where they might be going with her horses and were they not grateful for her hospitality.

The O'Leary brothers were quick to assure her that every drop of milk and plate of food had been most welcome and that they were indeed very grateful for the unexpectedly generous hospitality, only that they were keen to see their friends again and also they needed some money so they could continue on their way. They had hoped to sell the horses at Drumkeeran.

Their hostess gave a gift to each of them: to one brother she gave a purse with silver coins that never emptied; to a second she gave a fife and said that whenever he blew on it a fairy host would appear and do anything he required; and to the third brother she gave a cloak that would give him anything he wished for when he put it on.

She took back her own horses and went away.

The O'Leary brothers had little need now to make pots and pans and it is said they lived well for the rest of their lives, travelling over to Scotland to settle down – though much to the sorrow of the people of Kiltyclogher and district, who lost their favourite tinsmiths.

## A Fairy Good Deed

John Cullen was struggling to make ends meet and his last mare was too old to pull his plough. He tried to dig the land without the horse, but it was tough and tiring work. He had no money to buy a new horse.

One day, when John was out walking on the hills around Kiltyclogher, he met a stranger who asked him if he had bought his horse yet. John looked at the man in amazement.

'What makes you ask that?' John inquired.

'I know you need a new horse John. You can't plough your land without a horse.'

John lowered his head with embarrassment. 'Sure I can't but what does a man do if his old mare can't pull the plough and he hasn't enough money to buy a new horse? I've only my bare hands and a spade to get the land ready for planting and it's a tough call.'

The stranger told John: 'Go to the fair and buy a new grey mare.'

John stared at the stranger and replied: 'How can I walk up to a horse dealer and ask for a horse if I don't have the money to pay for one?'

The stranger looked deeply into John's eyes and it felt uncanny to the farmer. Who was this man? He looked at the stranger and tried to work out what his business might be and why he was so interested in – and knew so much about – John's predicament. He even knew John's name.

The stranger urged John to go to the next fair and pick out a grey horse that looked strong and fit for the hilly land of his farm. Then the stranger bade him goodbye and walked away.

John stared after him for a long time until he was lost in the shadows on the hillside.

A few days later John went to a fair and looked at all the horses. His eye was soon taken by a man walking on the street with a grey horse. John approached him cautiously and asked how much he wanted for the horse.

'£10,' came the answer. It was a fair price and the horse looked strong and fit for the ploughing.

John Cullen dug his hands into his pocket as he looked at the horse longingly. In one pocket his fingers touched something and as he drew out that hand to see what it was, he was holding a £10 note.

If the man noticed John's surprise at finding the money for the horse, he said nothing. The bargain was struck and John walked home delighted with his good fortune. He knew now that the stranger was a fairy helper and that this was a fairy horse. It would serve him well, as long as he looked after it.


## A Strange Weight on a Grave

A story from the 1700s concerns an old woman from south Leitrim who owned a shop for many years. It had been her custom to under-weigh goods, using false measures, to make extra money from her customers. People knew she did but no one ever confronted her about it.

When she died and was laid out for her wake, people saw the weights strewn over her bed, but when they tried to touch them to remove them, they disappeared. As if this wasn't disturbing enough for the family, things took a stranger turn when she was buried.

On the morning after her funeral, relatives visiting her grave saw the false weights again, this time lying on top of the freshly filled-in grave. Not wanting other people to see the weights there, nor understanding how they could be on the grave, they picked them up and threw them into the nearby lough.

The next day and the next, the same thing happened – yet each time the relatives threw the weights into the lough they reappeared on the grave the next morning. It was obviously a useless task and the relatives decided to leave them in place, hoping that they would eventually be covered over by the grass.

This is indeed what is said to have happened, with people forgetting to look for them when they visited her grave. But, the story lives on and perhaps is a salutary reminder that what we do in life may well still haunt our story after we are long gone – and there's nothing we can do to stop it, save changing our ways before we die.

## REFERENCES

**Tom Feely's Son:** Reprinted in full with permission from UCD. NCFS189:43-47; P J Rooney (60), farmer, Glenade. Gleann Éada school. Teacher: Bean Uí Mhaolaith.
**The Fiddler and the Fairies:** Based on story in NFCS193:9; Frank Fox, Lisnabrack, Manorhamilton. Cill Rúise School.
**The Fairy Pipers:** NFCS201:196; Thomas Nichleson, Dromahair. Collector: Patrick Joseph, Drumlease School. Teacher: Tomás Diolín.
**The Strange Beetle:** NFCS201:236. Drumlease School. Teacher: Tomás Diolín.

**Stone Deaf:** created from an idea in a story in NFCS189:76; Patrick Clancy (20), Glenague, farming. Diffreen School.

**The Perfect Hostess:** NFCS193:402. Corra Cluana School. Teacher: Pádraig Ó Caomháin.

**A Fairy Good Deed:** NFCS193:406. Corra Cluana School. Teacher: Pádraig Ó Caomháin.

**A Strange Weight on a Grave:** NFCS 229:77; Michael McKeever. Collector: Mary McKeever, Druim Míleadh School. Teacher: Ailbeard Mac an Ríogh.

# 10

# WHERE MYTHOLOGY AND HISTORY MEET

## A LITTLE STORY ABOUT A BIG SUBJECT: THE TUATHA DÉ DANANN AND SLIABH AN IARIANN

*Looking for a starting point to write about the Tuatha Dé Danann (the peoples of the goddess Danu) is a bit like trying to choose the best path up a steep mountain. It is a very large subject about which a great deal has been written. I need only to just touch on it here because of an association with Sliabh an Iariann, one of the highest mountains in Leitrim. If you want to read more, there is plenty material out there in books and on the internet!*

When the people of the goddess Danu arrived in Ireland, it is said they came in dark clouds, landing on the mountains in the North West and bringing a darkness over the sun for three days and three nights, according to Lebor Gabála Érenn ('The Book of the Taking of Ireland'). By the time the mist cleared there was no evidence of how they had arrived – whether by ships on the sea or indeed ships from the sky, as some legends say.

When they emerged from this mist, they were carrying harps, not weapons.

Some say their ancestors were the Nemedians, who had already lived in Ireland, or on what are now the islands off the west coast of Scotland, before the islands separated, but that they had been banished by the Fomorians. They fled to Greece and formed different tribes. When the first descendants of the Nemedians returned to re-claim Ireland, they were known as the Fir Bolg.

And when their distant kin, the Tuatha Dé Danann, made their return, the two groups met to try to negotiate how to live together. The options were for the Fir Bolg to give up half of Ireland or to fight. They chose to fight and they met at Magh Tuireadh.

The Tuatha Dé Danann's king, Nuada, lost an arm to the Fir Bolg champion, Sreng. No longer being 'unblemished', Nuada could not continue as king and was replaced by Bres, a half-Formorian, who turned out to be a tyrant. With miraculous skill, the physician Dian Cecht replaced Nuada's arm with a working silver one and he was reinstated as king. Dian Cecht's son, Miach, added magic to the surgeon's talent and recited a spell which caused flesh to grow over the silver prosthesis, but in a fit of jealous rage Dian Cecht slew his own son.

In turn, Bres was not happy to lose his new position as king. He complained to his family and his father, Elatha, sent him to seek assistance from Balor, king of the Fomorians. The Tuatha Dé Danann then fought the Second Battle of Magh Tuireadh, this time against the Fomorians. Nuada was killed by the poisonous eye of the Fomorian king, Balor, but Balor was then killed by Lugh, the champion of the Tuatha Dé Danann, who took over as king.

The final challenge came when a new wave of Mediterranean invaders, the Milesians, arrived in Ireland. They were delighted with the richness and prosperity of the country and travelled to Tara to meet the three men who shared the kingship at the time. On their way they encountered the three queens of the Tuatha Dé

Danann, Ériu, Banba and Fódhla, each of whom asked that the island be named after them.

When the Milesians arrived at Tara, they were surprised to find the three kings, Mac Cuill, Mac Cecht and Mac Gréine, quarrelling amongst themselves. They challenged the kings to give up the land or fight for it. The three kings asked for a truce of three days, during which the Milesians would lie at anchor, nine waves' distance from the shore.

The Milesians complied but the Tuatha Dé Danann created a magical storm in an attempt to drive them away. The Milesian poet Amergin calmed the sea with his verse, then his people landed and defeated the Tuatha Dé Danann at Tailtiu.

When Amergin was called upon to divide the land between the Tuatha Dé Danann and his own people, he cleverly allotted the portion above ground to the Milesians and the portion underground to the Tuatha Dé Danann.

And to this day it is said – by those who like a good story and believed by those who honour these ancient tales – that the Tuatha Dé Danann went into the underworld at Sliabh an Iariann, the iron mountain, becoming the people of the Sidhe, the fairy, and that they are there to this day waiting for their time to re-emerge.

## THE GOBÁN SAOR

The Gobán Saor is reputed to have been a highly-skilled architect and builder. Stories about him are found in old literary references as well as traditional sources across Ireland. He is associated as a builder of many of the early places of Christian worship, as well as great castles for kings in Ireland and England. Many parts of Ireland lay claim to him, but his precise date and place of living are lost in the mists of time. Mainly, though, he is placed in the late sixth/early seventh century. The *Catholic Encylopedia* considers him an actual historical figure born at Turvey, near Malahide,

about AD 560. He was canonised as St Gobban and it is said that
his fame as a builder in wood and stone would exist until the end
of time. There is little doubt that his exploits and cleverness, as
well as his highly sought skills, became legendary. The story that
follows is a mixture of many of the tales that roam the land.

### The Skin and its Price – or, How to Find a Clever Bride for a Less-than-Bright Son!

Gobán Saor's skills as an architect were greatly sought-after and he
was commissioned to build castles not only in his own country but
also across the sea in England. He spent much time away from home
and once, when he was away, his wife gave birth to a daughter.

Now, it is said that the Gobán Saor had long wished for a son who
could be as wise as he and who could be taught the many skills for
which he was so well known. So when his wife saw that she had a
daughter, she was dismayed. A tramp woman with a newborn son
happened to pass the house and the Gobán Saor's wife persuaded her
to give up the baby boy and exchange him for the newborn baby girl.
The tramp woman agreed and when the man of the house returned
from his project he was delighted to be presented with his new son.

However, as time went on he began to doubt whether this child
was really his, as the young boy did not seem to be picking up the
lessons his father was trying to teach him. The Gobán Saor decided
that a good way to find out would be to give his son some tasks to
do, once he was old enough.

It happened that the Gobán Saor was invited to go to London to
do a big project for a king, building the grandest castle in the whole
of England. He decided to take his son with him, but not before put-
ting him to the test. The great man was keen to ensure two things:
that his son was married to a wise wife and that his property would
be well looked after at home during their long absences.

Already, many eligible girls had been invited to their home and
shown the family gold and silver. Many remarked that a woman
coming into that household would never want to work. It could

be said that such women might not be trustworthy enough to look after so much wealth.

No women matched up to the exacting criteria of the Gobán Saor until the day he set his son a peculiar test. He killed and skinned a sheep, gave the skin to his son and told him to take it to the market and to bring home the skin and its price. The son at first thought his father was joking, but soon realised he had to do as he had been bidden.

Standing at the market with his sheepskin, many people came to ask how much he wanted, and when he replied, 'The skin and its price,' most of them laughed and went away … until late in the evening a young girl asked the same question. After he had given her his answer, she took the skin, cut off all the wool, and then gave the skin back to the Gobán Saor's son, along with the value of the wool she had taken.

Pleased with the sale, he returned to his father to discover that the wisdom of the purchaser was exactly the sign that the Gobán Saor had been looking for. Her cleverness was what he wanted in his daughter-in-law.

The Gobán Saor went back to the market with his son in search of the clever girl. She was invited to their house and when she was shown all the treasures she said, 'They are good and very good, only keep adding to them.' This was enough evidence for the Gobán Saor to be confident of his choice of daughter-in-law, so the marriage took place.

Soon after, the Gobán Saor and his son set out on their journey to London to begin work on a new palace for a king. They hadn't gone far when the Gobán asked his son, 'Can you shorten the road?' The son was perplexed and said to his father he had no idea how to do that. Immediately, his father turned back on his route and headed for home, much to the son's confusion.

That night the new wife asked her husband why they had come back so soon. When he explained, she had an answer straight away. 'Next time he asks you to do this, start telling funny stories and jokes. You will realise that this will shorten the road and your father will be pleased!'

Soon the journey began again and, within a short while, Gobhan Saor asked his son the same question. Immediately the son began to regale his father with funny stories and jokes. This time, the Gobán Saor did not turn back but continued on his way, just as the daughter-in-law had forecast.

When they arrived in London, the Gobán Saor told his son to give the impression that he was unmarried, as it might be useful to him. Once again, the son could not fathom why the father would say this to him, but he obeyed.

They started to build the castle and the king visited the work regularly, insisting that it must be the best castle in the world. When it was almost completed, the cook in the castle overheard a conversation between the king and some of his counsellors, discussing a plan to murder the Gobán Saor and his son when the work was finished so that no other king in the world could command the Gobán Saor to build an even grander castle.

The cook felt sorry for the young man and told him what she had heard. The son told his father and the Gobán Saor had to think of a way to protect their lives.

One day, the king asked the Gobán Saor if this was indeed the finest castle he had ever built and the Gobán Saor said it was. However, he pointed high up at the top of the gable and told the king it was a pity there was a black thread hanging over the stone. The king, not wanting to have a single blemish on his beautiful new castle, asked the Gobán Saor if it could be removed. After some thought, the Gobán Saor said that, to do this, he would need to use some special tools he kept in a trunk in Ireland. He told the king that only the king's son could go to get them.

The king agreed to send his son, so the Gobán Saor, to safeguard his life, wrote a message in an unusual language that not many people knew – his daughter-in-law being one of the few. Of course, when she read the message she knew immediately that the Gobán

Saor and her husband were in danger. She invited the king's son into the house while she opened a deep chest and began to look inside.

She asked the king's son: 'Do you have longer arms than me? I cannot reach down deep enough to find the special tools.' He stooped into the chest to search for them and straight away she pushed him in and closed the lid, locking it.

The wise and clever daughter-in-law wrote a letter to the king explaining that his son was locked there and could not be allowed to return to London until her husband and his father arrived home safely. The king saw that there was no other way to get his son back so he had to let them go and they arrived safely back in Ireland.

Some say that the clever and wise daughter-in-law was none other than the Gobán Saor's real child, as she was the one with all the right answers, and this is why he made sure she was married into his family.

## THE BLACK PIG'S DYKE

Archaeology is often the domain where mythology and history meet. What is handed down through folklore and the oral tradition for hundreds, if not thousands of years, emerges with new understanding when archaeological remains are examined and set into a time line through innovations like carbon dating and dendrochronology (tree ring dating).

That which survived over the centuries as a satisfying story can still remain as such to people who love stories and don't mind how literally true or not they are. On the other hand, for those who thrive on facts and like to know precise time and place as well as scientific explanations, the advances of our time provide new narratives to meet such desires.

The extraordinary high, double-ditched earthwork, which is known by many names, including the Claí na Muice Duibhe (Black Pig's Dyke), is one such example where a myth has been given new understanding through archaeological survey. This massive feat of engineering is 24m wide and up to 9m high in places. Remnants of it can be found in Counties Leitrim, Longford, Cavan, Monaghan and Fermanagh. Sometimes the Dorsey enclosure at County Armagh and the Dane's Cast in County Down are considered to be part of it. There are similar constructions in other parts of Ireland, such as the Claibh Dubh (Black Ditch) in County Cork.

In Leitrim, remains of the dyke can be seen from Lough Melvin to Lough MacNean, near the villages of Rossinver and Kiltyclogher. In neighbouring Cavan, there is evidence of it at Dowra.

One of the stories in Irish folklore claims it was created by the tusks of a huge black boar which tore across the country until it was finally captured. Another version is that it was a huge worm or ollphéist and this refers to another of its names, the Claí na Péiste (worm's ditch).

The ditch is no longer continuous, but contemporary historical and archaeological surveys are finding more evidence to back up earlier guesses that it was an ancient fortification separating the old kingdom of Ulster, or Ulaidh as it was known, from the south. It was substantial not just because of its earthen density and size, but because it was more than likely entirely strengthened from

the outside by a hefty oak palisade made from whole oak trunks wedged deep into the soil and connected to horizontal timbers.

And what is more incredible is a theory that the entire length of this possible ancient boundary was fully burned to a cinder all at once, in a remarkable destruction which may be linked to the end of the reign of those whose kingdom had its seat at Emain Macha, or Navan Fort, in the present County Armagh. Of the archaeological surveys which have taken place at several sites, the evidence is now increasingly supporting this idea. Latest carbon dating results have placed its construction around 100 BC. It may have lasted four or more centuries until its demise, which may be anywhere between the third and fifth centuries AD, depending how the narratives are placed on a literal time line.

In mythology, Emain Macha was one of the great royal sites of pre-Christian Ireland. It would have been the capital of the Ulaidh, the people who gave their name to the province of Ulster. It is a large, circular enclosure, marked by a bank and ditch. Archaeological projects found evidence of buildings on the site, including a huge roundhouse, and of several burnings and reconstruction over the centuries.

The name is thought to mean 'the pair of Macha' or 'the twins of Macha'. Macha was a goddess of ancient Ireland associated with war, horses and sovereignty. A number of figures called Macha exist in myth, legend and history and all are believed to be connected to the same deity. She is described as a daughter of Parthalón, leader of the first settlement of Ireland after the flood. A second Macha is the wife of Nemed, the leader of the second settlement. According to tradition, she died either twelve days or twelve years – depending how time is interpreted in mythology – after arriving and was buried in Armagh – Ard Mhacha (Macha's high place) – thus giving her name to the city of Armagh.

The next known Macha was the daughter of Ernmas of the Tuatha Dé Danann, who appears in many early sources, often mentioned together with her sisters Badb and Morrigu. The three are often considered a triple goddess associated with war and are sometimes called the 'raven women'.

Macha Mong Rúad ('red mane') was a daughter of Áed Rúad and, according to medieval legend and historical tradition, the only queen in the list of the high kings of Ireland. She claimed the kingship on the death of her father and various battles ensued, in which she was the victor, involving men who did not accept her claim to sovereignty. It is told that she had the stronghold of Emain Macha built by some of her captured enemies and that she marked out the boundary with her brooch, explaining the name Emain Macha as eó-muin Macha (Macha's neck-brooch). Her reign is variously placed in the seventh century BC, the fifth century BC and fourth-third century BC.

The final Macha is described as the daughter of Sainrith mac Imbaith and the wife of Cruinniuc, a wealthy cattle-owner in Ulster. She appeared at his house after his first wife died and began looking after his children. As long as they were together, his wealth increased. When she became pregnant to him, she warned him not to mention her to anyone, but he boasted at a festival organised by the King of Ulster that his wife could run faster than the king's chariot. Of course, the king demanded not only to meet her but to rise to the challenge of a race, not appearing to be perturbed by her heavily-pregnant state. She won the race and gave birth to twins on the finishing line, and thus the name is associated with Ulster yet again through the naming of the kingdom as Emain Macha, or Macha's twins. For the purposes of telling a good story, the conflict of explanations between Macha's neck-brooch and Macha's twins is just a minor detail! The story goes that she cursed the men of Ulster to suffer her labour pains in the hour of their greatest need.

Beyond Macha, many other famous names are associated with the place known as Emain Macha. These include the poet Amergin, the great warrior Cú Chulainn, his wife Emer, a king of Ulster Conchobar mac Nessa, a chief druid Cathbad and Deirdre of the Sorrows, the most beautiful woman in Ireland and her lover Naoise.

The eventual overthrow of Ulster came in a series of entanglements between a high king called Fiacha Sroiptine, his son Muiredach and three brothers known as the three Collas. The brothers were bent on overthrowing Ulster and two of them that remained, after one was killed in a different battle, finally achieved their goal. It's another long story but the short of it is that, in their success, they destroyed Emain Macha – and maybe at the same time reduced to a cinder the oak battlements of the Black Pig's Dyke – the subject with which this story began. Perhaps here, then, came the end of Ulaidh and from its ashes emerged the new kingdom of Airgialla. And perhaps this happened around the early or mid-300s or maybe the 400s, but the chronology of early Irish historical tradition does not lend itself to such absolute precision.

There is always more to tell but it cannot be here, nor now. In olden times in Ireland the fires must have burned long and warm to keep the listeners listening, for the stories are never-ending and, just like the flames, the names become hypnotic and all-consuming – as well as compelling. For now, my telling is over.

## REFERENCES

**The Tuatha Dé Danann:** http://en.wikipedia.org/wiki/Tuatha_ Dé_Danann – which cites as its primary sources: *Lebor Gabála Érenn* ('The Book of the Taking of Ireland'), ed. and tr. R.A.S. Macalister (1938-1956 and 2009). *Lebor Gabála Érenn. The Book of the Taking of Ireland.* Irish Texts Society 34-5, 39, 41, 44, 63. 5 vols and index of names. Dublin: RIA; Mesca Ulad ('The Intoxication of the Ulaid'; the 'Ulstermen'), a narrative from the Ulster Cycle preserved in the twelfth-century manuscripts the Book of Leinster and in the Lebor na hUidre. The title Mesca Ulad occurs only in the Book of Leinster version. Also *Lady Gregory's Complete Irish Mythology* (1994) (originally published as two separated volumes in 1902 and 1904).

**The Gobán Saor:** NFCS189:129; Mrs O Connor (90), farmer's wife. Gleann Éada school. Teacher: Bean Uí Mhaolaith; also NFCS198:453; Brian Keany, Annagh, Glenfarne. Collector: Kathleen Keany, Broca School. Teachers: T Ó Chioráin, S Ó Gallchobhair; also NFCS224. An Clochar, Béal an Átha Móir; also various website references.

**The Black Pig's Dyke:** online article, 'Excavation at the Black Pig's Dyke', by Aidan Walsh, Clogher Record, vol. 14, no. 1 (1991), pp9-26, published by Clogher Historical Society. Other online material and book references.

If you enjoyed this book, you may also be interested in …

## Roscommon Folk Tales
Pat Watson

Roscommon has as many stories as there are people travelling its roads. Featured here are intriguing stories of a vanishing lake, Oileán na Sioga (The Fairy Island), and the miracles of St Kieran, along with darker tales of the battles of Queen Méabh, the Monster of Lough Rea, and the story of Betty of Roscommon, Ireland's first (and only) hang woman – not to mention the fantastical accounts of encounters with leprechauns, pookas and giants.

978 1 84588 784 1

## Clare Folk Tales
Ruth Marshall

A unique collection of traditional tales from across the county, which explores Clare's rich heritage of myths and legends. We will hear the tales of well-known figures, including Cúchulainn, Brian Boru and Clare wise-woman Biddy Early, as well as lesser-known characters such as Grian, Daughter of the Sun, and the Hag of Bealaha. Also featured are fantastic stories of mythical creatures and underwater worlds.

978 1 84588 761 2

## Donegal Folk Tales
Joe Brennan

Donegal has a rich heritage of myths and legends which is captured in this unique collection of traditional tales from across the county. Included within these pages are the tales of Balor of the Evil Eye, the Witch Hare, and Paddy the Piper. The reader will also learn about the legends surrounding St Patrick and St Colmcille, and extraordinary stories of ordinary people's encounters with devils, ghosts, silkies, changelings and fairies.

978 1 84588 767 4

Visit our website and discover thousands of other History Press books.

**www.thehistorypress.ie**

Hmmm, maybe I could do *one* more event...

# CHAPTER 15

# How to finish the Arc of Attrition

S o, as a bit of an expert now, I thought I should use my experience to help others and explain how to finish the Arc of Attrition.

Right. Here's my advice, the essential info all wrapped up in one thought:

**Just finish it.**

That really is all there is to it. But I'll expand a bit…

The coast path is a brute. When the weather is decent, it's just a more-or-less permanently undulating ripple on the edge of the sea, designed primarily to ruin your quads, your hamstrings, your adductors, your ITB, your calf muscles, your feet and… well, all the other bits I haven't mentioned. No particular section of the path is that high. No hill is too steep. The overall elevation gain of the race isn't too much. But a lot of not-too-bad all adds up, and when you're physically tired if you have some doubt, a low point, a struggle – the race will burrow into you and amplify all those problems.

But just keep going.

And if the weather is crap. If you have driving rain, gale force winds, and mud… so, so much mud! Then keep going. You signed up for this, right? You wanted to do it. You trained. You looked forward to it. In the middle of this hell, you've got no-one to blame but yourself.

One hundred miles is a long way. At some point it's going to seem ridiculous. It's going to hurt, mentally and physically. You'll be tired. A muscle or joint will shout very, very loudly that you have to stop, and your brain will ask you "why?" Why are you doing this? What's the point? Just… why?

But just keep going.

If you don't eat enough, you'll feel weaker than you should. Your mood will drop, the demons will sneak in through the back door and make DNF'ing a really pleasant option. So, take a gel, a packet of crisps, a flap jack or a Cornish Pasty, shove it in your face, force yourself to swallow and…

Just keep going!

There's a lot of hype around the Arc of Attrition – it's a difficult race, but it's taken on an almost mythical reputation. When you toe that start line, you need to have two things in your head. First: it's just a race. Along a path. With a bit of mud and a few hills. It's nothing to be scared of. And second: you must *want* to finish.

Although it is "just a race", it will take a lot from you – it will work every muscle, and it will pry at every crack in your mental state. When those cracks open and the questions about why you're doing it bubble up, you need a solid – no, and absolutely *incontrovertible* – reason as to why you **must** finish the race.

Just try and not make that reason because you've fucked it up 3 times before!

# THE END

**Before you go…**

I genuinely hope you've enjoyed this book. If you did and have a few minutes to spare, I would be so grateful if you could leave a review (hopefully positive!) on Amazon, and maybe rave about how amazing it was to spend a few hours getting lost in these pages to all your friends on social media!

You can stay in touch over at:

**www.swcpplod.co.uk**

and if you've got any questions or feedback, you can use the contact form or social media links on the site.

Thanks again for taking the time to read my book!

Printed in Great Britain
by Amazon

79773048R00129